farewells to plasma

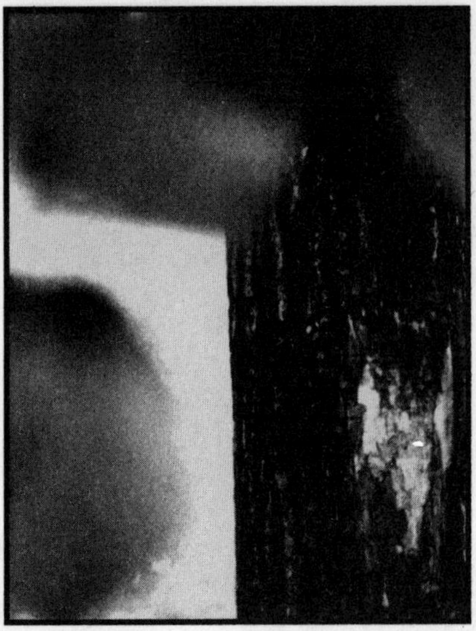

Natasza Goerke

farewells to plasma

translated from the Polish by W. Martin

TWISTED SPOON PRESS / PRAGUE 2001

This publication is financed in part by the ©POLAND
Polish Literary Fund from the resources of the Ministry of Culture
and National Heritage of the Republic of Poland

Copyright © 2001 by Natasza Goerke
Translation copyright © 2001 by W. Martin
Illustrations copyright © 2001 by Jeffrey Young

All rights reserved. This book, or parts thereof, may not be
used or reproduced in any form, except in the context of reviews,
without written permission from the publisher.

ISBN 80-86264-15-7

table of contents

Waiting Underground (Transitions)	11
Tourists	18
Beyond Fear	20
Siddhartha	21
Stories	22
Linen Shops	23
A Plot	25
Celtic Cross	26
Umbrella	28
The Thin Arm	30
Segment	31
Different Schools of Perception	32
The Visit	33
The Return	35
Siberian Palms	38
Rocking Horse	44

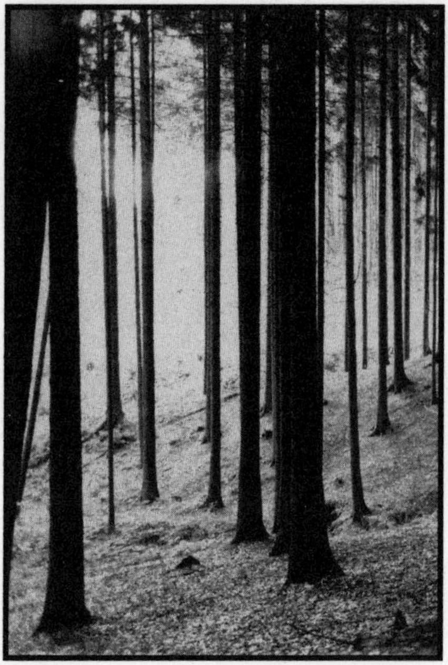

Konstantin Musk's Last Feint	51
For the Sake of Art	58
Zoom	65
La Mala Hora	70
Waning Luster	80
Farewells to Plasma	87
A Wonderful Day in May	93
Respite	95
Catharsis	98
Marchand	103
Dog	113
Kumari	121
The Final Defeat	126
The Chosen One	127
Art Diabolica	129
Translator's Note	137
About the Author / About the Translator	141

waiting underground (transitions)

The moment Virginal Patience felt the tickling between her third and fourth ribs, the bed grew fragrant with the smell of grapevine, a crow flew off the windowsill, and a pencil slipped out of a hand asleep on an abandoned rebus and struck a light bulb, causing a circuit to short. So the delivery took place by candlelight, and the fact that the girl emerged from her mother's side was interpreted generally as a hallucination caused by the darkness. The darkness was likewise credited with a host of other phenomena accompanying the birth: hieroglyphs falling like rain from the ceiling; the smell of loose-leaf notebooks roasting; a willow's heart-rending sobs; the whinnying of a winged pony; and the reveille a sad elephant played on its trunk, which ended abruptly the moment the doors to the chamber opened and the on-duty doctor walked in.

"She's a heavy one," the doctor said, weighing the baby in his hands.

"And a March baby, too," sighed the midwife.

"But for that, she's exceptional, unique, the most beautiful child under the sun, the smartest and most capable, too. She was created for a purpose neither of you can ever dream of!" Virginal Patience thundered, snatching the girl away from the doctor. "I'm naming her Mousy Wousy," she declared, "and someday she'll be a pharmacist, just like me."

The moment Virginal Patience uttered these words, the girl's fingernails curled into talons, her eyes flashed, and from her mouth erupted a geyser of profanities so precise in their metaphors that they withered the doctor's heart, while the midwife's face lit up with a curious, thoughtful grin.

Where there's a name, an identity can't be far behind.

Mousy Wousy's unfortunate name saw to it that she was a plump, rosy-cheeked, and suspiciously well-behaved little girl. She had big eyes, long eyelashes, and blonde locks whiter than cotton. Like a paté-fattened goose she meekly gulped down the protein supplements forced on her, and without a shadow of disgust allowed herself to be kissed and pinched by slobbering aunts and ladies from the neighborhood. In short, Mousy Wousy was a perfect little doll, and her future was looking more pastel every day.

It was only through love that the miracle of her transformation ever came to pass. And it was a first love, too — something that always differs from its successors the way one May differs from the next.

Mousy Wousy got paler and skinnier; a black devil soiled her blonde locks and her soul. As she turned through a world that for all its low protein levels made even less sense, she looked at her anemic, cherubic self in the mirror and declared: "As of today, I'm Patti Smith."

"And as of today, I'm Elvis," a boy said. "Elvis Costello."

Thus they concluded their alliance. Not long afterwards, Patti Smith wrote her first poem. The word *darkness* occurred in the poem eight times; *why* occurred five; *ass*, three (in the locative); and *never* and *always* thirteen times each. The poem was titled "Love," and Elvis Costello wrote music for it that drowned out all the words.

To be dissatisfied with dissatisfaction is the blindest of alleys, and that's why, in one particular century and one particular cultural context, the safest option for rebellious (as well as mechanically inept) children has been either psychology, sociology, or the noble discipline of Polish philology. Such a desperate choice is as salutary as it is ruinous. The children are prevented from sliding into the abyss of marijuana abuse, and they also cease to associate with controversial artistic elements, such as painters, poets, psychiatrist-gurus, owners of poppy plantations, fashionable schizophrenics, cultural innovators with pedophilic tendencies, or punk rock musicians. Mornings in the Old Town suddenly stop seeming so cool, the guitar begins rotting in the garage, and the awful question as to whether Sid Vicious could even read and write threatens with the power of ridiculousness to shake the old world from its foundations. What takes its place isn't so much a more perfect world, as this one's new and sophisticated negation.

Public enemy number one: a poorly defined nothingness brings its hazy countenance into focus, the rebellion finds its object, and those who were children not long before vent their fury onto this most concrete of opponents. Dissatisfaction with life's shallowness gives way to dissatisfaction with phonemes — it's the gender of rhymes that irritates, and sestinas, triolets, and Sapphic strophes that instigate battles. The notion that a poem of Tuwim's is in iambic tetrameter with feminine line endings, and that the lines (also tetrameter — a first) in *Konrad Wallenrod* are dactylic, can make the delight in reading poetry disappear for years, leaving in return only sadness, glasses, and the yearning for a lost paradise.

Patti Smith was happy in her unhappiness. Nothing repulsed her more than library reading rooms. With hands yellowed from wringing, she would leaf through volumes yellowed from age, but their contents interested her less than the rapt faces of her studious friends. These friends — the bright future of academia, the hope of literature and the bane of up-and-coming writers — drowned their rare moments of doubt in the ocean of tea they drank over books. During reading breaks they would devote themselves to learned debates, the contents of which disturbed Patti Smith far more than they amused her, and inspired her, as she lay curled up under the table, to write her next line: *Waiting underground.*

An underground is a mirror for the city.

The Dalai Lama is the king of Tibet. He has no crown, but he has a palace from which he escaped forty years ago. The Dalai Lama is an ordinary monk whose extraordinariness lies in his having repeated for forty years a single sentence: *I'm waiting underground.*

The Dalai Lama's underground is a mecca for diplomats, artists, and politicians who crave the light. They enter the kingdom of the mind with their ties on, because it's only the highlanders in Poland who cut off their guests' ties after they enter their houses. They simply don't like them is all, and what's more, these days they can afford the extravagance. Polish highlanders take pride in their pride and are shrewd about marketing it, and their music and folk dances guarantee that Bavarian or American tourists allow their ties to be cut off without a word of protest, afterwards even tapping their feet to the fiddles and eagerly drinking mead from hand-painted mugs. Tibetan highlanders have much in common with their Polish counterparts and are similarly good at business. Both the Pope and the Dalai Lama are great for sales. There's only one difference. While the highlanders of a free Poland sell hand-painted eggshells, Tibetan highlanders use their colorfully painted shells to smuggle out messages. These messages read: "Free Tibet." Tourists are held in high esteem there, just as in Poland under Soviet rule tourists from the other side of the so-called iron curtain were held in high esteem. Who can say what a "Free Tibet" will actually be like. Maybe when Tibet is finally free, the formal differences will disappear as well. They'll have a so-called normal life, a thriving business of hand-painted eggshells, a parade of desires awakened after long slumber, and an exuberant snipping-off of ties all around.

And the Dalai Lama, quietly meditating underground.

"Your name will be Transcendental Happiness," the Elder Lama said. He threw a white scarf around her neck, set a figurine of the Buddha on top of her head, and whispered: "Write, and remember that all beings, even critics, were once your mothers."

Transcendental Happiness felt her heart fill with transcendental happiness and wrote a story for the occasion. It was an extremely short story, rhythmical, and so condensed that it could be read only in installments, a word at a time, at bedtime.

Traveling in the imagination isn't the only way to grow, and although an American transcendentalist would have cast his veto on this point, Transcendental Happiness wanted to prove this to herself empirically.

Smuggling the relics of a certain Too Difficult Love in her heart, she walked out of Indira Gandhi International Airport in New Delhi, plunged into the motionless air, and along with others came to a standstill in the stagnancy of bodies standing still. She was not waiting for anything and she had no plans. And as she had no map, either, she did not know where she was; and as she did not know that tigers eat people, she was not afraid of the tiger. The ground really was, as she imagined it would be, red, but other than the color of the ground, nothing agreed with her Rabindranath Tagore-inspired image of India. When she had had enough of watching the motionlessness, Transcendental Happiness wiped her damp forehead with the sleeve of her T-shirt, threw on her backpack, and began moving in the direction of what she correctly surmised was a bus. The bus had neither windows nor a driver, but it did have metal seats, and after squeezing into the narrow space between a portly Sikh and a goat, Transcendental Happiness sat down on a white-hot skillet. What better way to heal the soul's affliction than through that of the body! How negligible the wound in the heart becomes when one's butt is being consumed by fire! Transcendental Happiness accepted the pain with the dignity of a wizened ascetic, and since she also took a lively interest in landscapes, she pulled out the little bottle of gin she'd gotten on the airplane, exchanged it for the seat beside the window, and with her heart growing ever lighter, she looked out happily on the future.

Tell me what you think of India, and I'll tell you who you are.

"India is my personal affliction," lamented the monk Thomas Merton.

"India is Maitreya," blushed the writer Mircea Eliade.

"India is a land of art, poetry, dance, and music, of experiences equally new and fascinating, like Japan," beamed the diplomat Octavio Paz.

"India is a region alien to our Mediterranean culture," grunted Józef Pszczoła, occupation: Pole.

"Avoid contact with children; disinfect the chairs; secure yourself to your bed at night with a chain; by day go out only in groups; and under no circumstances return a smile," Transcendental Happiness read in her German guidebook, and realized that her days were numbered.

Wanda Rutkiewicz, R.I.P., was once well-known in the Himalayas. She scaled the 28,000-footers one after the other, but for certain reasons she was never well liked in Poland. Her Polish Himalayanist colleagues taught the nomad children how to ask for candy: "Say 'Wanda pussy' and the candy's yours, kid." After that, the children would yell "Wanda pussy, Wanda pussy" at the sight of any white woman, and maybe Wanda Rutkiewicz herself even heard it. But no one will ever know, for the sentence has outlived her.

After she returned from India half a year later, Transcendental Happiness wrote her next story. By no means was it an account of her Travels in the Orient. It was a short story about how Wanda made a painting. The painting was very colorful at first, but later all the red in it faded away, then all the green, then the blue, and the black, and in the end even the white. What remained was emptiness, an inviting space through which forms and contents, dreams and intentions, wonder at the ephemeral nature of existence, and the ephemeral nature of that wonder, all flickered.

"Where are you from?" asked the scrawny waiter in the little hotel in Darjeeling.

"From Poland," Transcendental Happiness proudly replied, to which the waiter held out his hand and whispered entreatingly: "Wanda pussy . . ."

Wanda is a name that in the land of the inheritors of Mediterranean culture is associated not only with a tragic Himalayan mountain climber but with a tragic princess in a certain tragic Polish legend. Transcendental Happiness, being a typical Pole, identified with both tragic figures.

"I'm Wanda Wanda," she realized, and with dignity accepted her tragic fate.

"I'd sooner drown myself than marry a German," she cried, quoting Princess Wanda, and like her predecessor threw herself into the Vistula. But she immediately regretted her decision. The water was cold, and her fiancé, who was standing on the bridge, cried out: "Wanda pussy! Haven't you read Heraclitus?"

We'll assume that the mortified Wanda Wanda got out of the water, married the German, and established a wonderful precedent in Polish-German history.

tourists

In the beginning, the guide paced back and forth.

"That, ladies and gentlemen, is Kanchendzonga," the guide announced. "Look at it quickly, for any moment it might disappear. And I can assure you, Madam, its disappearance will disturb you greatly." With that, the guide shrugged his shoulders, snapped his fingers, and Kanchendzonga disappeared.

A commotion set in.

"Ladies and gentlemen, please, control yourselves," the guide said. "Here we have a cloud. Please, take a look, for in a moment it, too, will be gone. And I can assure you, Sir, its absence will leave you gasping." With that the tour guide sighed, snapped his fingers again, and the cloud vanished.

The tourists were dumbstruck.

"Ladies and gentlemen, please, do not block the walkway," the guide was growing impatient. "We must keep an observation area free for the next group. If you don't hurry up, we won't make it to the fourth hill to the right of the meadow in time to see the *pretas*." "What sort of *pretas* do you mean?" the astonished tourists asked in unison. "Big ones," the tour guide assured them, and they set off for the hill.

"Ladies and gentlemen, there they are, the *pretas*," the guide announced, holding out his hand toward a lake. "We can't see anything," the tourists said, peering into the smooth surface of the water. "Just as I thought." The guide shook his head, looked at his watch, snapped his fingers, and disappeared in the forest.

Exasperated, the tourists scattered in disarray across the field, while from the forest a voice resounded: "Ladies and gentlemen," it said, "we have prepared a special attraction for you today. In a moment we will find ourselves in a meadow filled with *pretas*."

The voice came closer and closer. And with it, eyeing the meadow with their lorgnettes, the next group of tourists.

In the beginning, the guide paced back and forth.

beyond fear

A little stone began falling down the southern slope. In the course of its fall, it grew bigger. "What's this," Sherpa Tenzing asked, shifting anxiously. "Another avalanche maybe?"

"No, it's just a stone falling," Sir Edmund Hillary replied and, without taking the toothbrush out of his mouth, mumbled: "What, are you afraid?"

"Me afraid?" Tenzing guffawed. "I'm beyond fear!" And he, too, began brushing his teeth.

When they finished brushing their teeth, they both started to whistle, and then Sir Edmund Hillary struck up a conversation. "Hey Tenzing," he joked, "if we make it to the top, you'll go down in history just like the Queen." "Oh, you're making that up!" Tenzing laughed. "Do you know what 'sir' means in Nepalese?" "No, I don't," Sir Edmund conceded and took out his notebook to jot down the new word. "'Sir' means 'head,'" Tenzing explained, and they both burst into laughter.

A stone was falling down the southern slope. "O Himalayas," Sir Edmund thought to himself. "Someday I'd like to see England," Sherpa Tenzing sighed, and then he, too, lost himself in thought. The snow was knee-high, so they kneeled.

The stone rumbled as it rolled down.

"What are you looking for?" Tenzing asked, watching Sir Edmund rummage in the snow. "It took my toothbrush," Sir Edmund mumbled. "Oh that's too bad," Tenzing commiserated, and they both burst into tears.

siddhartha

He had an extremely difficult personality. When he was born, it was raining.

Maybe that was why.

He was always falling asleep. He probably never really ever woke up.

A genius, but sick, the doctor's wife concluded. It's only a phase, the doctor reassured her; it'll pass, just like when his voice changed.

It did not pass. He kept sleeping ever more deeply. And so peaceful. But asocial, the lady at school whispered with embarrassment. He never hits the other children, he never plays soccer. He only talks to this one other boy.

Why are you always with that Govinda, the doctor's wife asked angrily. It's not right, especially with so many girls around.

But he said nothing, he just cried a little and fell asleep.

He's depressed, the doctor suggested and retained a specialist. I'll snap him out of it, the specialist promised. Heh heh, he smiled craftily and without any warning pricked the boy's finger with a needle. Blood flowed out, but the boy slept on.

And he kept bleeding, sleeping, a blissful smile on his face.

The bandages didn't help.

Sir, Madam, your son is a hemophiliac. The specialist washed his hands, bowed quickly, and left. So he's not a homosexual after all, the doctor's wife jumped for joy and was immediately relieved. Don't be so sure, the doctor reprimanded her, thinking about heredity.

But he also quit nagging the boy.

And so, more or less, did the boy pass his youth. And adulthood.

He slept and slept; he slept through the doctor's passing away and the doctor's wife's long illness, and his own old age.

It wasn't until he was just about to die that for one moment he opened his eyes. O Govinda, he sighed, the rain never stops, the dream never ends, maybe we screwed it all up. And he was gone.

stories

Story #1, "Breakup": I broke up.
Story #2, "Memory": I remembered.
Story #3, "The Comeback": I came back.
And so on.

The stories are short, but concise. No need to scrutinize them. The final sentence is contained in the first. Saves all sorts of time. Who cares about the rest. All that paper in between. There's one for everyone. Narratives, inventories, notes. Read it ages ago.

And the fact that I was breaking up? That I remembered? That I was on my way back? Who hasn't heard it all before! A label is enough: an abbreviation, a title, any old crap, and all at once it all comes back.

Remembers. Breaks up.

Whoever doesn't get this, he'll never figure it out. No matter how he scrutinizes it. All those sheets of paper in between. He won't figure out what it means. To break up, to remember, to come back. And so on.

linen shops

1.

My face was wrinkled, gray, and what's more, it had no shape. "God, what is that?" my mother would think to herself, and just to be safe she never took me anywhere, not even to my aunt's. One time, though, she had to: My aunt had died.

My mother took a long time putting my face in order: She smoothed out the folds, creased the edges, she even slapped me a few times to give me color. But my face was unusually stubborn and flaccid. "Not a dog, and not an otter either," thought my mother, cracking up; she flicked the ash from her cigarette and accidentally singed a hole in my forehead. "Oh would you look at that, he even has acne," she said, and took a bedspread out of the wardrobe. "Here, cover yourself," she ordered, and ran off for a comb.

I covered my face with the bedspread; my mother carefully combed out the fringes for me, and we left for the funeral. "You have a fine boy there, Maria," my uncle complimented her, and added as he wiped the tears from his eyes: "The very picture of his dear, departed aunt."

2.

My identity was a synthesis of all the colors of the rainbow: It was white. Likewise, the edges of my existence kept losing definition and gradually merged with the edges of the forms surrounding me on all sides. Finally, it happened.

"I spilled," I whispered, and ceased to exist.

"You're such a pig, those linens were brand new," my wife cried out and looked at her watch. "Spread the blanket out," she said, "I'll give you a fresh one after the show." Then she turned on the TV.

A mirror was shining on the TV screen.

3.

Saturday was linen-changing day. By Sunday we were already looking forward to it. "Not long until Saturday," we would think on Monday and cheer up, and in this way our weeks would pass.

We knew, of course, that what's bred during the week will come out on the weekend, so naturally we never forgot to sleep. "You've slept in your bed, now you'll have to make it" we would say to ourselves, and since we wished to waste no time, we always went to sleep right after waking up.

On Saturday, well rested, the whole family would go shopping. The shop was white. It smelled like starch and filled me with dread. It was a linen shop, and entrance with ice cream was strictly forbidden.

a plot

I met a four-legged old woman in the village. She had three heads and five hands. They claimed that at a distance she could recognize a cause, that she was Baba Yaga.

I greeted her politely as was my custom. "Greetings, Baba," I exclaimed, "there must be something in the air today, for my eyes have been watering since morning!"

"There's nothing in the air today, it must be in your eyes," countered Baba Yaga, and then, having dropped the cause, she removed to the woods at a gentle trot.

"That's no Baba," I could see for myself. "That's a mare," I whispered to the man standing next to me. "So what did she say to you?" asked Maciej.

I was chilled to the bone. Maciej had eight heads and seventy hands.

In the village they claimed that he was Baba's accomplice, a Forefather.

Only now do I understand.

celtic cross

For years I've whiled away the tedium of Sunday afternoons in the Natural History Museum in London. My eldest sister, Eileen, always thought I must be a masochist. And who knows, perhaps she was right.

It was Sunday.

"Let's go for a spell to Portugal," my pale sister Eileen proposed and stared at my mouth. I deliberated. "No, I'll never travel anywhere," I decided, and Eileen left the house without a word. Shortly thereafter, having given the children over to my younger brother Simon, Eileen left us. Shaking a rattle, Simon sighed: "Shit, man, Eileen went back to the North."

I will forever associate Eileen with the North. It was Eileen who, still sucking her thumb, once dragged me from my crib and under cover of night thrust into my hands my very first bottle of petrol. "Let's go avenge Daddy," she whispered and looked over at the bed. On the bed, with her cheek nestled in the arm of a Celtic cross, Mother was snoring. The cross was embroidered on an enormous satin pillow that Mother brought to bed every night in place of our father. Ever since the day a bomb had blasted bits of our father all through the church, our mother had become quite distrustful. She boarded the windows and would refuse to shut an eye until our simulated snores had given way to measured breathing and the occasional sleepy whimper. Only once did Mother fall asleep first. It was the very night that Eileen pressed the bottle of petrol into my hands. Moments later, my two older bothers, Paul and Patrick, fell off the rusted gutter on the front of the house, shot down by unidentified (as the newspapers later reported) perpetrators. I was eleven years old at the time, and at the funeral, holding on tight to Eileen's frigid hand, I resolved to become a priest. Shortly thereafter, Mother decided to move us away from Belfast forever.

I became a gardener, and Eileen soon married. I'll never understand what induced my sister to marry a Protestant blighter like her husband. As a bachelor, I had little right to voice my opinion in marital affairs; thus, I observed in silence as Eileen tried to reconcile two mutually exclusive moral worlds. Wanting to feed both the wolf and the lamb at the same time, she would tirelessly plant bombs in Bob's company car, then immediately afterwards, spurred by marital duty, inform the London police. Once, however — and it was exactly on the twenty-first anniversary of Paul and Patrick's death that it happened — Eileen neglected to call the police, and Bob left us with a bang and without ever knowing the cause of his death.

The cause was truly unsavory. For several years, Bob had been having an affair with my younger sister Kathleen. Burdened with guilt, Kathleen called the entire family into the room; without a word, she doused herself in kerosene and walked over to the fireplace. I'll never forget the frenzy in Eileen's eyes as she stared at Bob. Bob lit his pipe without a word, and Martin, Kathleen's husband, packed his bags and went back to his mother in Belfast, without even saying goodbye to the children. We stopped hearing from Martin, and it was only recently that Eileen, vegetating as usual in front of the television, noticed his shoe. It was lying next to the detached leg of a terrorist. Eileen turned off the television, calmly took a small bundle out of the desk drawer, and disappeared into Bob's garage.

It was Sunday.

"Let's go for a spell to Portugal," Eileen proposed, pale as ever, staring at my mouth. I deliberated. Lying on Eileen's bed was an enormous satin pillow that gleamed with the carefully embroidered profile of Cromwell. "No, I'll never travel anywhere," I decided, put my hand in my pocket, and released the catch on the grenade.

As on every Sunday afternoon, I made my way at a leisurely pace to the Natural History Museum in London.

umbrella

The narration will drag on into infinity, but the man to whom I owe the most important moment of my life is P. Hammer-Hammer. The permanent state of non-realization I glimpsed on the pale face of P. Hammer-Hammer one day in an umbrella shop revealed to me what hours of introspection in the company of the most sought-after mirrors in the world would not have been capable of revealing. And although many, many days have passed since that moment, I'll never (never! never!) forget the expression on P. Hammer-Hammer's face.

I caught sight of P. Hammer-Hammer on a July afternoon, in, let's say, an umbrella shop on the corner of Cesar Hoop Street. The umbrellas are just for decoration, props that allow me to redistribute the weight of meaning and arrive at that crucial moment when P. Hammer-Hammer showed me his face.

P. Hammer-Hammer did not even notice that I had come in; he was lost in thought, looking for an umbrella. The salesman was smiling just like any umbrella salesman would smile on a sunny July afternoon, but P. Hammer-Hammer took no notice of that smile; he was lost in thought, looking for an umbrella.

July, afternoon, an empty shop with, let's say, umbrellas and the three of us: a salesman, P. Hammer-Hammer, and myself. I don't remember which one of us was the most non-present.

Practically petrified, I stood before the vitrine, and without a word (of course) fixed my gaze on the pale face of P. Hammer-Hammer. I observed the way he finally picked out an umbrella (which was merely a prop, decoration for the moment to happen in), politely allowed the salesman to wrap it in finely patterned paper, and — with a thrilling expression of permanent non-realization on his pale face — carefully signed the check with his hyphenated (why?) last name.

Throwing me a blank look, P. Hammer-Hammer carelessly slipped the checkbook into his pocket, picked up the umbrella, and without a word (of course), walked out of the shop.

Sometimes the devil shows up in the mirror, proof of everyone's worst fears about hell; all of a sudden, the suppressed grimace succeeds in adorning your familiar face. Unexpected, a surprise, a blow to your third eye. This is how the devil shows up in the mirror.

I caught sight of the devil on a July afternoon, in an umbrella shop, let's say. Get out! Get out! I thought and, sensing his pale face on me, indifferently picked out an umbrella.

With a smile on my face (and oh what a smile, my God!), I walked with the finely packaged umbrella out of the shop, and with the checkbook clenched in my hand, made my way without a word (of course) up Cesar Hoop Street on a July afternoon.

And the narration? The narration will drag on into infinity. Days will pass. Hundreds of days will pass, each of which could just as easily never come to pass, or pass in the opposite direction, or pass me by and happen for someone else entirely.

And this is something I've known for certain from the moment I saw the face of P. Hammer-Hammer.

the thin arm

It happened to her right arm.

Her arm swelled up from the shoulder to the wrist. "It looks like the work of a demon," they whispered. "She must be possessed."

Whatever it was, her arm (along with the demon) kept swelling. She looked like a balloon. A picture corroborates this: A ballerina sitting hunched over, one arm around her right knee, a balloon around her left.

Due to the paranormal nature of the situation, they considered appealing to a magician. Unfortunately, the white magicians had washed their hands of the affair (they fled in a panic), and the black magicians didn't want to get their hands dirty (so they kneeled).

The magicians' behavior was an unequivocal testimony to the demon's power. No one knew how to act.

The problem took care of itself: One day the arm exploded, along with the rest of the body. It was the quietest of explosions: No sudden boom, no clamor of panic; simply within minutes the room filled up with a three-dimensional face, expressionless, hair streaming from it like rays from the sun.

Sir James Frazer, Cambridge anthropologist, performed the definitive diagnosis. He concluded: It was a three-dimensional jaundice, the aerostatic demon of melancholy, nesting, as it tends to, in skin and bones; the primitives still believe in its existence.

segment

A man was sitting in an armchair drinking tea. His face was hidden in the cup. A lit candle on the table indicated that it was autumn.

Yes, it was autumn.

Leaves stuck to the windowpane, raindrops pelted the night and drummed rhythmically against the sill, a flower withered in its flowerpot.

The man stretched from head to toe. He was one hundred eighty-two centimeters long. Time passed.

"Good day," I said, and the man pulled his tired face out of the cup.

His face looked familiar to me. Leaves were floating down the windowpane, autumn was raving on the sill. I tried to crack a joke, but it upset him.

Crammed onto the line of my life, the man sat motionless and:

(a) Muttered: "We should talk about who's being isolated here on whose line."

(b) Called out: "Knock it off, you're not a line, you're a circle, and the cyclical nature of your problems is wearing me out."

(c) Said nothing.

Whatever it was, the flower withered in its flowerpot.

different schools of perception

He was a chewer all his life.

"Stop chewing so greedily, try savoring the taste a little less crudely — suck it," I implored him, but to no avail: Leopold chewed.

"I savor as I chew," he mumbled. "You have no idea what you're missing by sucking."

I thought about it.

"Leopold," I said, "maybe there's some kind of strength in chewing, but it isn't enough to fathom the essence of the taste. The only way to raise yourself to a more refined niveau of sensible experience is by sucking."

"Oh please, please: Suck it!" Leopold laughed maliciously, put on a record, and started chewing.

A string broke, the earth began to quake. Sir Yehudi Menuhin ostentatiously snapped his bow in two, walked out of the record, and yelled: "Hey guys! When will you stop mistaking me for sirloin and start listening?"

the visit

> *The place, her posture's grace, the taste of her apparel*
> *All transformed her so, she was unrecognizable.*
> — A. Mickiewicz

Sir, you are so delicate, I feel I must give you my coat and light your cigarette.

I hold the door open for you, I pull the chair out for you to sit down, and at the sight of your new hairdo I am rendered speechless. You tell me that you feel like a woman inside, and naturally, I believe you, Sir. What's more, I am trying to help you get in touch with the woman inside you even more, that is, all the way. I'm sure that as a woman you won't lose your nerve.

To start with, I'd like to ask you to take off your panties. That's right, only your panties; the sweater can stay. I promise not to look, but as soon as you've taken off your panties, please be so kind as to march your naked ass over to that chair by the window, the one that's on an incline and looks like a sort of ironing board — imagine that. When you sit on it, the chair will make sure your head stays below the rest of your body, and most importantly, below your legs. I'm sorry, but your legs will have to stay up in the air. Do you see those two indented, trough-like dishes, Sir? You'll have to put your knees in them. It's not difficult, it's just to keep you from doing backward splits up there. Can you manage? Okay, so now I'm walking up to you and initiating a conversation. Of course you can't see me, Sir. The only thing you can see is the wall behind you. But not to worry, I can't see your face either as long as my head is more or less level with your ass, which is nothing unusual after all, since none of this is about you, Sir, or about having a conversation with your face, but about it — your ass — and about giving your ass a thorough examination.

So then, I begin the examination. I smile at your ass, and talk to it noncommittally, and in general do whatever I can to get you to loosen up. Now and then I allow myself a little joke or two, you understand, nothing malicious, Sir, not at all, more of a compliment than a joke. I tell you that you have an incredibly tight, how shall we say it, anus, which doesn't surprise me. I've seen all kinds of anuses in my life, and you, Sir, God forbid, have nothing to be ashamed of. Especially since I am a doctor, and tight, shall we say, anuses aside, I am quite skilled in inserting into your ass the latest advances in modern medical technology: tubes, rods, cone-shaped lenses, tweezers, cameras, tiny bats, anchors — in short, everything they've come up with to perfect the penetration of your interior. And at the end, Sir, I insert into your ass my finger in order to determine organoleptically whether any pustules have sprouted on the wall of your, ahem, anus.

And you, Sir, of course, are lying there the entire time very patiently, trying not to think, or trying to think about some especially pleasant topic — about how great it is to be a man, for instance. If you don't know what to do with your hands, Sir, simply hold your arms up against your sides. Next to your hips you'll find two metal handles. Should you by chance happen to feel any pain, you should hold on to those handles very, very tightly.

Yes, you are now emitting your femininity so powerfully, Sir, that if I were a man, I would love you to death.

the return

I knew I had become a woman again. My true form delighted me, and I moved in it as freely as an actor trying out a new type of experiment. Contact with other men was a purely occupational pleasure. I knew perfectly well what men were like, and I sensed how their presence inspired the continuing improvement of my work. But I have to admit, it was women, as usual, who were the true mystery for me. I observed their cunning professionalism, how they used their bodies to operate. I examined how they carried themselves, sounded out the nuances of their sophisticated mimicry, and slowly I mastered on my own their technique of bursting into heart-rending sobs, plunging other men into feelings of distress and irrational guilt. Just like the women, I recognized the higher value of cool calculation, and I spent so much of my time fabricating appearances in order to make an impression that I was completely unaffected by the sin of rational thinking. In keeping with my role, my eyes grew ever wider and more expressive of a deep melancholy; my lips filled out into innocent little cushions; the naïveté of my views moved others to tears; and my inability to walk home alone through the but-look-how-dark-it-is streets activated the immediate enterprise of all the other men around me.

With virginal countenance I received homages to my delicious femininity. I suspect I sometimes identified with my role too strongly for my own good: with all the requisite vacuity, I got involved in a romantic relationship with a certain starry-eyed philosopher. I let my guard down and for three years allowed that hypersensitive, hopelessly incompetent person to lavish flowers and poems on me while the elbows of my knit sweaters became so worn they began to look like cobwebs. Of course, while the role of muse was certainly a feather in my professional cap, eating beans from a can and pickled cabbage every other day was hardly so ethereal. Evidently my hair began to lose its luster, and with professional goodness women began passing on their half-used jars of face cream to me. I could feel myself slipping out of character. Attacks of fury followed one another with ever-shorter intervals, my mouth took on a sneer of resentment, and at the slightest provocation my little hands would clench into brutish fists. Just as I was visibly losing control over my feminine attributes, I felt myself losing power over the man with whom I shared my life. He hardly ever sent me flowers anymore, and increasingly he took off for weeks on end. It wasn't until I was forced to borrow money from a sympathetic girlfriend for my solitary consumption of beans and cabbage that I finally woke up. One evening, I stepped down from the stage for a moment and uncovered my real face. I hurled words heavier than any stone. I threw away one mask after the other. And in the morning, after gathering into my once-shiny handbag my make-up kit and the sad debris of my remaining accessories, I walked out of the apartment of that haunted, spineless wretch with my dignity intact.

All alone in a rented room, I launched an exhaustive revision of my role. The great taste of experience was the promise of my success.

My next husband turned out to be an ideal audience. He appreciatively applauded my every performance, which in turn inspired me to develop new and ever more daring productions. He responded flawlessly to the situations I stimulated, writing off his infrequent criticisms to his own dilettantism in the fine art of understanding women. Like a true gentleman he never cast suspicion on my talents. He would indulge me sympathetically by stroking my again-lustrous hair, and when I turned my delicate shoulders toward his sentimentalism, he would proudly tense his muscles. Evenings, he would peel tangerines and patiently explain to me the operative principles of both the electric chair and electric razor.

With my freedom growing day by day, I traveled through ever-newer regions of my burgeoning femininity. Purely as an experiment, I permitted myself the occasional enrichment of playing with the fire of controversy. To be sure, my innocent face was an unusual accessory to the emancipative slogans of feminists, but the memory of beans and all those poems was a sober reminder to me not to dig my own grave frivolously. In the end, I decided to take part informally in the activities of a few charitable organizations, and my astrology and dowsing classes provided me with friends who responded sensitively to the treasures they discovered in my no-nonsense personality.

I had become a young and universally well-liked woman. But it became abundantly clear that I was not to perform this role all the way into my gray-haired and kindly old age.

I don't know what happened to make me notice her.

There was really no way for me to recognize her. She had a large, masculine body, and it was clear that her performance as a man was flawless. And still, I recognized her at once . . .

Exposed by her penetrating gaze, I wanted to escape, just like I always used to do. To leave her — maybe for the rest of her life — in tears. This time, though, escape was impossible. I understood that the same power that had nailed her to me was now compelling me to follow her. With horror I realized how attracted I was to her new hairy body — and so without a word of protest I allowed her to slap me on the ass, and reconciled to my role at last, in mincing steps, I hurriedly followed her home.

siberian palms

Reality for John Pinstripe, Jr. was a string of difficulties. At age two he fell out of his baby carriage. At age five he swallowed a watch. He was albino, and his milk teeth grew unevenly. As a child he stole, lied, and tormented animals in secret, and his favorite game was spitting. He would spit on a wall until it softened, then gouge holes in it with a nail. As if that wasn't enough, his father, John Pinstripe, Sr., was a chief accountant.

Of his mother, all that is known is her name, Joan, and that she always looked through the peep-hole before opening the door.

John's relations with both parents were unfortunately quite chilly: Pinstripe, Sr. was cold on account of his career, the mother on account of her nature, and Junior could not help but be influenced by his home.

Neither were they well-off; the mother, who had all she could do to make ends meet, wrapped herself in a scrap of shearling and sobbed: "How can I get these ends to meet when my hands are freezing?"

Well, life wasn't easy.

"Nothing's easy," declared John Pinstripe, Sr. and fell silent. And with time it became clear that Pinstripe, Sr. had nothing more to say. There were times of course when he would vary his pronouncements; at times he would throw out some uncompellingly cheerful remark, something like: "They beat us 2-1;" "Flooding in India;" "In Africa, flu."

The infrequent conversations between Joan and John Pinstripe, Sr. looked something like the following:

"I don't understand," said Joan, "why our grapes come from Ghana." "It's so we'll have a ready market for the banana," replied John, Sr. "But we don't have bananas here," snapped Joan. "What do you mean we don't? I just saw some," said John Pinstripe, Sr., shrugging his shoulders; he opened the newspaper and sighed: "Drought in Mozambique."

At the sight of Junior, Senior invariably furrowed his brow and threatened: "If you don't sit up straight, you won't get dinner."

It's not surprising that John Pinstripe, Jr. grew into an aloof and apprehensive man. He lacked friends, but he did not lack for desires, especially the desire to fly.

"You've inherited an awful lot of problems," sighed Billie.

"I've inherited a lot of problems," John Pinstripe repeated, and glumly surveyed his immediate surroundings.

John's immediate surroundings comprised a shelf with books, a window, a *ficus Benjamina*, and a bathtub. It was in the bathtub that John started writing poems to Billie K.

A poem by John Pinstripe for Billie K.:

A unit of forest is a tree
A unit of speech is a word
But what is Billie a unit of?

It was clear of course what Billie K. was a unit of, but John preferred not to say the word "space." "Does literalness change things?" he would ask himself. "Can the key to space be contained in a word?"

"Yes," whispered Billie unexpectedly. She began flapping her wings and took off from the windowsill, calling out: "On the condition that you set the word free." Billie K. was a pigeon.

Under the influence of the above occurrence, John, Jr. drew a bath and wrote one of his more dramatic stanzas:

In images I fall asleep
In dreams I fly away
Why do I wake with my shoes on?

As it turned out, the road to answering the above question would be a long and rocky one, fraught with humiliations.

Nevertheless, John Pinstripe, Jr.'s reality, generally understood, was increasing in space. And, oh! — the way it felt inside was the wing of Billie K.

For Billie K. had decided to give John wings. "Genes schmeens," she muttered, "Your shoes are what's keeping you down. Who says the sky has to be blue, grass green, and that palm trees can't grow in Siberia?"

John Pinstripe, Jr. nearly died of astonishment: He started to choke, he went red, then he started turning white; but he didn't turn completely white — at the last second he stood on his head and crossed his legs, and perceiving the world from this unexpectedly new perspective, he calmly began to analyze his own poems.

He began with a basic definition of poetry. "Poetry," he argued, "is the totality of ornaments that determine the shape of the road leading the poet away from madness. How do my verses look in this regard?"

"My verses don't look so great," he observed. "They don't lead me anywhere, they only intensify my madness, they're full of ornaments that rather than growing along the road grow over it instead."

"This is awful," insisted John Pinstripe, Jr. and spontaneously jotted a three-liner down on a napkin:

An accountant father
A mother named Joan
Where did the son come from?

It was the beginning of a huge metamorphosis, the search for his roots on earth, the dramatic inquiry into his identity.

"I'm Icarus," John, Jr. declared somewhat infelicitously, and, taken aback by Billie's laughter, put his hand over his mouth. ("So who isn't?" Billie asked.)

It was only the usual bragging of a neophyte, the paradox of any bantam pilot; nevertheless, at close range, John really was something of an Icarus: He flew up, then fell down, flew up, fell down, flew up, fell down. "There will come a day when I don't fall," he vowed.

That day never came. Preoccupied with the search for his own identity, the younger John Pinstripe evidently distanced himself from the world of mundane phenomena. Or to put it another way: In the world of mundane phenomena, he was present only in spirit, which — in contrast to those who were bodily present — made him invisible.

But isn't being invisible the same as being absent?

"Nes, I mean, yo," John replied, managing, by scrambling negation and assertion, to avoid taking a concrete position. "I mean, let's take these genes as an example," he sighed: "A chief accountant for a father, a mother named Joan: it should all be perfectly clear, cut, and dried. Then all of a sudden the son starts shivering in the cold, feels himself sinking under the weight; but then, the second the doorbell rings, he rushes to the peep-hole. Is this the power of the genotype, the invisible force that for that reason is all the more a presence in one's life, no matter how much it is resisted or denied?"

Nevertheless, John Pinstripe, Jr. was obstinate. "The day will come," he repeated, "when I'll spread my wings and recognize myself automatically."

And as a matter of fact, although this may sound like a novel with its necessary sequence of events, that day really did come.

"It's all about opposition," John Pinstripe, Jr. realized at dawn. "I'm full of the genes of my impassive parents, and as quickly as possible I should invoke antigens against them, seal up the peep-hole, sever my bonds with the earth, and fly off after Billie. Then I can leave all my fears down below: My fear of Pinstripe, Sr., my fear of tradition, my fear of a sham existence."

"Ha," smiled Billie K. "There's your automatic self-recognition, which is the first step toward self-consciousness, which is the beginning of self-acceptance. John, you have set foot on the path of progressive self-development."

"Why of course, I'm developing myself," John Pinstripe, Jr. acknowledged modestly, went to the bathtub, and counting out the syllables on his fingers, translated the essence of self-development into a poem.

The essence of self-development as presented in a poem looks like the following:

With no sense of nonsense
A Siberian palm
Has given birth to a snowman

"Self-development," John, Jr. explained in a commentary on the poem, "means both to reduce all mental habits to the level of nonsense and to learn how to forget. You need to get it out of your head that you in any way resemble anyone, or that anyone has genetically conditioned you. The next step is forgetfulness — first forget everything you've been taught about palm trees and bananas, then forget who they wanted to teach. By now you will have attained the mental state of a Siberian palm. You'll perceive all the J. Pinstripe, Sr.'s as completely unthreatening (and, for that reason, perfectly agreeable) genotypes, and you'll recognize yourself as a schema-free absurdity, and, irrespective of any obligations, you'll begin to bear fruits that contradict healthy logic — you'll laugh tears, you'll warm yourself in snow, and without getting out of your bathtub, you'll wander beyond the orbit of the senses."

"What about me?" said a disquieted Billie K., "What about your poems?"

"I'll continue writing poems," John promised. "You, though, are the shadow in this space. I'll make you longer or shorter — an experiment on the durability of my projections." "Bravo," Billie applauded, "Bravo. You've answered the question about causes. But what about effects?"

A unit of space is a pigeon
A unit of a poem is a word
But what is John Pinstripe, Jr. a unit of?

It was clear of course what John was a unit of, but the word "evolution" shouldn't be abused.

Here the tale breaks off: John Pinstripe, Jr. standing on the windowsill, smiling and dropping flower buds to the ground below.

"But how will I make ends meet if there isn't any end?" wailed Joan Pinstripe. "A plague has broken out in Ghana," replied John Pinstripe, Sr.

There is no other point to the story.

rocking horse

The sixteenth day of winter had ended. The weather was frosty, the birds had all gone off to hell, and one by one across the so-called sky Lufthansa-held angels sped past.

The angels weren't my idea; they were Solomon's, a man who never played the game, but lost anyway. Irrevocably. Forever. And there's nothing that I, nor anyone, nor anything, can do to break that spell.

"I'm dying," Solomon informed me one morning when the weather was still warm, birds were chirping, and on the linden tree in the garden aging leaves fluttered briskly. "Unfortunately I don't believe in resurrection, and I don't know what will happen afterwards."

Afterwards, there was the afternoon: the September sun crept for a moment into the room and inspired Solomon with the desire to live, then it hid itself again behind the clouds. It lasted just a moment.

"But after all, I might even live another ten years," Solomon suddenly changed his mind and flashed me a look of reproach. "Why don't you say something? Even you once told me how every moment is both an end and a beginning and how that's precisely why we're alive, whether in the forest, or in the city, the experience of death has never abandoned us . . ."

Solomon was right: the experience of death was a constant companion. We fell along with the leaves, we withered with the ladybugs, we scried infallibly in the eyes of lovers and monarchs the approaching dusk; only for ourselves were we never capable of foretelling anything. Too faint-hearted to build the house, yet still not carefree enough to do without it — we wandered incoherently through the salons of the real, and although life spread itself out under our feet like a divan, we gave ourselves over all the more to detours down roads of no substance strewn with abstraction.

"Darling, I'm in Calcutta!" I informed him on the phone the day we were supposed to fly to go mushrooming together in Norway. "I've learned how to juggle tangerines, and now I have a job performing for the leper children in Mother Teresa's orphanage."

"Good lord, a stone's fallen from my heart!" said Solomon, relieved. "I'm off to Toronto in a little while for a conference, and I had no idea how to let you know."

No, we were definitely never bored. Whether that was because of the permanent impermanence of places, or the inevitability of returns, or perhaps due to something else entirely — I don't know; in any case, the uncertainty of the future tangled itself up perversely with its inevitable obviousness, and we felt increasingly exhausted.

"But maybe we could so completely change our context and live our lives somewhere where the only sure thing is that nothing can ever be known? For example, your country," thought Solomon out loud while cutting bread. "Tell me, are there flowers there? Poets? Streets? Is there something people truly believe in? Something they cultivate?"

I thought about it. In a way, Solomon was right: a radical change of context might really be a good thing, like observing from the window of an airplane the lover who had just betrayed you. But had we already fallen so low ever to escape so high?

"You know, I don't really know" I said unenthusiastically. "As far as flowers go, my country is like a pair of lotuses: in one of them, you sit patiently and dream forever of the other one growing out of the ground. But unfortunately, nothing does grow; there's no way — not that tradition, not that soil. And that's why the population placed its bets on geese husbandry. There, too, an ancient custom demanded that at year's end the carp be clubbed to death with pickaxes, and it wasn't even that long ago that they still hung the shot hares up in their windows at the onset of spring. At the moment the situation is undergoing changes, at least in the cities: you can buy carp in stores now, like anywhere else, already dead, and instead of hares hanging out of windows, they have satellite antennas. And as for the streets . . ."

"Oh, how awful," interrupted Solomon. "Has the populace of this remarkable country ever encountered other cultures?"

"A few, yes," I murmured. "Why?"

"I'm just interested to know if they've ever heard anything about, say, Africa?"

My heart withered, my stomach began to turn; the eastern roots, which had produced the western flower, quivered uneasily, and an avalanche that had been set off continued on in the same way.

"About Africa?" I listened to my dangerously teetering voice. "But yes, of course . . . You know, in our elementary schools the children learn all of Soyinka by heart, in tears they read of the bloody history of Biafra, and on the playground, of the thousands of other battles, it's the war of the Yoruba and Ibo they reenact . . ."

Solomon covered his plate with a napkin.

"Oh, so people there know how to read!" he shouted and clapped his hands. "By any chance have they ever heard the name Shakespeare?"

Unable to stop myself, I burst into tears.

"My dear, out of love for the Elizabethan period, every fifth woman takes her bath feeling just like Ophelia, and every other man behaves like Falstaff!" I shrieked, wiping away the tears. "The names, to be sure, have undergone a local modification and are assimilated to native rules, and so they sound a little different . . . Żosia, Tadeusz — you understand, a hundred vowel mutations, two hundred restrictions. But the source is pure . . ."

I was plunging ever deeper, but I knew that I was doing it out of a double-sided love: love for my country, which horrified me, and my love for Solomon, which horrified me even more. Loves like that, as if there weren't enough suffering already, were mutually exclusive.

"And are these enlightened people aware of the role Marlowe played in Shakespeare's life?" whispered Solomon, clearly distressed, offering me a napkin. I wiped my nose and fell silent; this time the question stung.

"Unfortunately, Solomon," I began quietly, "in my country, you could find God for centuries in church, but the truth still hides in public restrooms."

Putting down the sandwich, Solomon shot me a look like the just-assassinated Martin Luther King.

"The frog is an androgyne," he informed me sadly. "A wingless prototype of the angel; sometimes man attempts to follow his tracks, but unfortunately human law as a rule is an outrage to angelic nature."

"But the poets submit to God's law!" I thundered with conviction and, rushing in where angels fear to tread, added: "Shakespeare, Rimbaud, Auden . . . It's abundantly clear: it's the frogs we have to thank for our most beautiful poems!"

Solomon stood up from the chair, shook the parmesan off his nightgown, went to the telephone and made his decision: "I'm flying to Johannesburg. I'll fax you a sonnet from the plane."

One can live the thought of tomorrow. One can live the thought of yesterday. As for me, I lived exclusively the thought of Solomon, who — without having shaped my past or promising the slightest hope for my future — was the purest incarnation of every Zen master's most pious wish: he lived exclusively Here and exclusively Now. At times white, at times black, he passed on with each passing moment, before which there was no way to predict if he would reappear with the next. And if so, in what color? Will I recognize him?

"The frog is a flawless creature," I repeated with the obstinacy of an atheist shouting out his gnawing doubts.

"And so you won't leave me? You won't sever the silver spiderweb that connects the antipodes like a tremulous meridian?" Solomon asked me and turned his head in disbelief.

No, I wasn't intending to cut the silver spiderweb constituted by our enormous feeling, distilled from the erotic, of friendship. I'm just not sure if we always distilled this friendship correctly. Why, once from Kathmandu, where I was working with Tibetan nuns on the roof of a temple in the sun, I sent Solomon some flakes of skin I had peeled from the back of my neck while making incense; Solomon then sent me, from Tel Aviv, where he was organizing a conference on the issue of peace in troubled nations, a detailed account of the proceedings along with a pair of his own underpants. I hung the underpants on the plank bed in my narrow cloister room, alongside the censer and the statue of Buddha. Time, however, worked decidedly to our disadvantage — the nuns stole the underpants, and the peoples of the troubled nations kept mutilating their governments.

We felt increasingly at a loss, and over our union a developing feeling of guilt cast its shadow.

I admit, I was tired and at times I desired to escape. But knowing full well that nothing leads to proximity better than distance, I instinctively drew nearer. And it was true: observed from up close, Solomon resembled the cheek of Naomi Campbell diffused under a microscope.

"We're both executioner and sacrifice: we're witnesses," he informed me one afternoon and stared out at a landscape sunk in fog. "Do you see what I see?"

Why yes: I saw that I could see nothing.

"Clouds," I murmured. "But we at least have Consciousness . . ."

Solomon walked away from the window and, closing his eyes, pronounced the following:

"Went down to the harbour and stood upon the quay.
Saw the fish swimming as if they were free:
Only ten feet away, my dear, only ten feet away."

The tears glistened on Solomon's cheeks.

"Darling, it's only a poem, You already know freedom is always only ten feet away," I assured him, hugging him. "You carry it in your heart alongside all the other dreams. Sometimes you live for it, sometimes you fall, but if you don't know how to either live or die, then you can simply try to describe it."

"Describe it? So much has been said about freedom, it's enough to make citations!" snorted Solomon. "It's just that the history of the world is in truth the history of slavery, which every white poet, no matter how great, would prefer of course to forget. My genes, however, make sure I'll always remember. You understand — it's killing me . . ."

Fortunately for me, my genes, however different, guaranteed the same thing. Genetically or not, we've inherited a fragmentary consciousness, which, in preventing comprehension of the whole, has deprived the afflicted fragments of any rest at all.

"Solomon, perhaps we can try to get beyond conditionality?" I moaned helplessly. "Let's sever ourselves from the roots, change our context, and begin from completely virgin territory to write our own history . . ."

Solomon looked at me in disbelief.

"Virgin? You talk about virginity while the last dikes are cracking open, violence overwhelms virtue, and any minute my immune system might lose its last duel with catarrh?" he shouted. "Go back to Calcutta, my dear, go back. And if you're in the south sometime, give my best to Jerusalem. As for me, as long as it isn't too late, I'm flying off to Belfast for a meeting with a certain, never-before-translated poet . . ."

Watching him leave, I lit the incense without a word. Not for any of the gods, though; the gods, after all, although we believed in them each in our own way, long ago gave up believing in us.

I lit the incense because it smelled like the forest.

Some time later a letter arrived. Not from Belfast — from Berlin.

"I'm dying," wrote Solomon, without indicating the reason for his visit to Germany. "I don't believe in resurrection, and I don't know what will happen afterwards."

Afterwards, the last leaf fell from the linden tree in the garden. The sixteenth day of winter ended; the birds all went off to hell. Sitting on my suitcase, I stared at the frozen sky, across which one by one, as if nothing had happened, Lufthansa-held angels sped past.

konstantin musk's last feint

He was not, unlike other intellectuals, stingy.
— Paul Johnson

The art of writing is difficult, and few can attest to this better than Konstantin Jirzi Musk.

He was born the only child of Victoria and Longinus Musk in "a land situated at the edges of the great civilizations, where wolves still roamed freely, but smallpox had been eradicated, an achievement of which every citizen was duly proud." His parents were in no way exceptional: Longinus was a train engineer, Victoria a ticket inspector. They traveled a lot.

While his classmate Hans Hansen was plucking chickens under the rotting thatch, the young Konstantin would sit waiting in locomotives, eating hard-boiled eggs, and making mosaics out of the broken shells. In time this prematurely acquired liking for eggs would become for Konstantin what plucking chickens became for Hans — a pernicious habit.

Musk, like Hansen, was timid and wore galoshes, and his trouser pockets were always full, too — though with eggshells, not feathers. But there was more they had in common: they both were right-handed; neither had any use for women; and each of them felt that life was an obligation, which, like love, was best fulfilled then gotten out of. They both believed in reincarnation, too. Hansen insisted that Musk was the incarnation of a troll, while Konstantin claimed that Hans would come back as a hen. At school they shared the same nickname: "Quisling."

They both would become the greatest writers of their time.

The atmosphere in Musk's parental home was nothing like the "sauna filled with offspring" that another of his great countrymen, Henry Battle, once called it. Konstantin's cousin Joanna Musk claimed that, "Our home was a rusted tin in which everyone was desperately trying to play some kind of role." Konstantin's role was "to dust the credenza and scare away advancing bailiffs with his looks." At the sight of a bailiff, Kostek "would throw himself at the newcomer's feet and in a terrible croaking begin to recite his own version of Piccaut's well-known strophe:

> *Old fusel to him seems youngest must,*
> *A swine to him seems a windmill,*
> *To him rope looks like facial hair,*
> *And an egg like a boy both good and fair . . ."*

In moments like these the confounded bailiff "would toss Kostek ten cents and take pains to avoid touching him as he hurried out of the house."

As we can see, Musk's accomplishments are even more remarkable if we consider that he was doubly untalented. For not only did he suffer a lack of any poetic gift, but in contrast to Hansen, he had no social skills either. And it was not only bailiffs he frightened away, but women, too. As his biographer, Paul Millieu, has suggested, "[Musk] had something of a frog about him. At the sight of a woman, he would squat down, stick out his lower jaw, and emit croak-like noises. And he was always rattling the eggshells, too, which were always tumbling out of his pocket. But he acted the same way at the sight of men."

Konstantin Jirzi Musk was not, in fact, a beautiful person: his torso was too long, his limbs too skinny, and his acne-spattered forehead had over the years become a source of tasteless jokes for other children and adults alike. "When I lectured on the structure of volcanoes, I recommended that the children closely observe Kostek's face," the geography teacher admitted, and apparently Longinus Musk's favorite way of rebuking his son was to threaten him with: "Pipe down! Or

I'm calling the stork!"

It is hardly surprising then that Musk, Jr. came to distrust all expressions of sympathy. He suspected a trick behind every smile, and when he ran into schoolmates on the street, he would yell, "Why are you following me?" This suspiciousness developed as he grew older, and years later it found expression in his first novella, *Footsteps and Whispers*, the publication of which was hindered by an event that, while distasteful, was big with consequences.

The twenty-year-old Musk had sent his novella for evaluation by M. Ireni, a gifted critic who based all his judgments of literary works solely on their titles. Unfortunately, in reporting new titles to him, Irene Ireni misread that of Musk's novella as *Footsteps and Whiskers*, and as a result, the first chance he got, Ireni denounced Musk in all the newspapers as "a snot-nosed, second-rate Marquis de Sade." Musk brought suit against the critic, but, as is often the case, the charge of slander itself was the prosecution's best publicity. And so it has always been.

All at once hundreds of eyes and ears were directed at the scandalized debutant. The phone rang incessantly with calls from publishers. Lowlifes inundated him with letters and propositions. A television firm began producing a movie about his life, and renowned journals jockeyed for the rights to future works. As Millieu wrote, "Musk had gotten overnight what others labor years for in vain."

It should be added that at the time Musk had written nothing aside from one accidentally scandalous novella that no one (and here one must give a sigh of relief) had yet read. Nevertheless, our awkward frog was transformed overnight into "The Grand Pervert of Domestic Fiction" that all the newspapers were raving about.

Did Musk identify with the role imposed on him? Did the moniker "Grand Pervert of Fiction," which was to stay with him from then on, not have some basis in reality? Was the deformation of that titular consonant only an accidental surrendering of idea to ethos, or was it not perhaps as Millieu claims, that "in mistaking whispers for whiskers, Irene Ireni had guided the errant river into its destined bed"?

In analyzing the lives of writers, we tend to go along with the views of their biographers. Indeed, even Musk referred to his childhood dreams as "the stuff of a pretty good criminal, whose only failing was in having too many motives for the crime." In the same autobiographical note, he remarks, "I was born in a place rife with superstition, dread, and anathema; above the city, pale angels circled, gnawing at the pinions of all earthly dreams. They were called the guardians of morality." "Whenever I raped a girl in my thoughts, I would look up afterwards at the sky in fear. The bolts of lightning never actually reached me, but knowing about them effectively deterred me from committing the next rape."

Did Musk even then sense in himself his potential as a freak? This we do not know. There is no doubt he was a shy boy, unusually susceptible to an eclectic array of deviations. As a child he detested diapers, he ran naked through train cars, and as his cousin Joanna has noted: "He always put his aunt to shame." In time, Musk's exhibitionism became so well known that he ran away from home. It was a dramatic flight, recounted later in his well-known novel *Pride*, which is regarded by many oppressed minorities as an ideological manifesto.

He never returned home. He took up residence in the forest with a she-bear, which gave rise to further rumors, this time regarding sodomy. There are some who read into his late story "Fur" an explicit relationship with a bear, although there is no evidence that Musk really was a sodomite.

It is difficult to say how Musk's relations with women were handled. We do know, however, that his only documented relationship, with the then thirty-year-old journalist Helena Brlova, Hansen's future wife, definitely was not one of the successful ones. It is not known what Musk did to Helena, who years later declared that, "At the very least, Kostek is insane." Marta Lurpak, a friend of Musk's from his school days, describes in her diary another, equally enigmatic situation: "The guests all went home and it was just us. Kostek asked me to take off my dress, which I did. And then he started eating an egg. And that's how the night went. In the morning, I put on my dress and left, and he was still eating the egg."

It was no doubt apparent even then what the dominant feature of Musk's creative personality was: to seduce without seducing.

His marriage-by-correspondence with Hansen's seventy-year-old mother, Violet, had all the characteristics of a *non consummatum*, although how it was conducted remains a secret. Letters were the only form of contact for this atypical couple, and although it was said that Konstantin would "sniff at Violet's letters in intimate situations," this fact does not contribute much to our knowledge of the writer's enigmatic psyche.

Shortly after marrying Violet, Musk became famous for his "aesthetics of embryonic stages." He liked most to surround himself with two-year-olds, but there is no concrete evidence whatsoever to suggest pedophilia.

What we do know is that in his treatise "The Body and the Bioplast," Musk declared himself resolutely for the bioplast. "The natural development of all organisms can be attributed to their inevitable exhaustion," he wrote. "To keep an exhausted organism alive" is a crime comparable to "worshipping the chicken" while "ignoring the generative potential in the egg." In the essay "The Dignified Decline," which he wrote for the local evening paper *Ex*, Musk stated that "demography is a function of demagoguery," and that "long lives and long speeches in defense of them are equally uncivilized actions." In a letter to his then twelve-year-old friend Nancy Corp he wrote,

"It upsets me to see you so stubborn in holding on to life. [...] Do you really want to waste away the rest of your days a monument to yourself? A little dignity, Nancy, a little dignity!"

Succumbing to the fashion for prophetism, Musk, like Hans Hansen and Henry Battle, foresaw the exact date of his death. "I will live forty-one years," he confessed in a letter to his wife, "and the insolence of that fact justifies my mission." Musk never explains what mission he means. In a telephone conversation a year later, he confesses that, "These days no one trusts anyone over thirty," and "the only justification for a perversely long life" is, perhaps, "that children may be made aware of their priorities in forming a culture that has been ruined by sclerosis." It was at the "Symposium on the Family" that Musk uttered his famous "Once they've had children, children should go away," and on the Day of the Child he delivered a lecture in which he demanded for nursing babies unconditional access to the mass media. It was in these years, too, that he wrote his memorable "Polemic against Custom." "The law countenances no difference between a parent and a child," he asserted. "However, as regards the obligations that devolve upon them, there is a difference of principle: the former are to serve death, the latter, life." "May the word 'mother-in-law,'" he states in an addendum, "be a word without referent, and may maidenly love blossom unimpeded!"

His views were by no means exceptional. At the same time Musk was writing "The Body and the Bioplast," Hans Hansen was finishing his famous appeal to new recruits with the call "Praised be the infant!" and Henry Battle, who despite everything remains the greatest Byron scholar our times, when asked what he thought was the optimal lifespan, is said to have answered, "Twenty-nine years."

Battle's reply was elaborated years later by his then nine-year-old wife. "Of course, Henry was thinking of the optimal life-expectancy for men."

Henry Battle was wrong.

Konstantin Jirzi Musk died at the age of forty-five, having choked on an egg-yolk. Hans Hansen, who himself was to die two days later by suffocating on a feather, succeeded, not without reverie, in noting down Musk's last words. They went: "I don't want!"

for the sake of art

> *You don't know how true it is.*
> — A. de Verbaal

As a rule, a poet's imagination mocks logic, and the best example of this may be the famous words uttered by twelve-year-old Alfred de Verbaal at the sight of a pug stuffed no less than half a century earlier: "I remember, I remember how he peed." To no avail did his mother kick him in the shins and whisper in consternation: "But that's impossible, my boy, that's impossible . . ."

The boy not only did not take back his words, he plunged in even further, assuring everyone there that "it was an unusually sweet little pug that would only sleep on [Alfred's] lap." The consequences of such behavior were to be near fatal for the future laureate: His tongue was ripped out, and his parents, fearing further scandals, put him in a dungeon that was, as he himself later wrote, "Impenetrable to everything but the shouts of passing jugglers and the occasional whiff of perfume." Bound in chains, prevented from turning by the shackles, he could look only straight ahead; what he saw "weren't things, but their deceitful shadows." De Verbaal spent his whole life in the dungeon; it was only a year before his death, that "to the great horror of those present, and in defiance of the customary resistance of matter, he rose up into the air and filtered through the ceiling into the garden above." After a brief consultation the deed was deemed a miracle, and Prince Ulf, the garden's owner, presented him with "a shed and peasant woman, six rolls of pressed paper, two quills, and a gallon of ink." Thus equipped, de Verbaal "pinched the peasant girl, but finding no satisfaction in this, he returned her to the prince. Then, without wasting any more time, he sat down to write." As is well known, he did not waste that time at all. His works, the result of a year's effort, were hailed as "the best joke since the idea of God."

As we can see, Alfred de Verbaal's genius had developed his whole life under abysmal circumstances. Yet, did not his cruel fate turn out in the end to be rather paradoxical? Why, the poet himself insists that if he had not lost his tongue and been thrown into a dungeon, he would have abandoned himself "to philosophical speculation, conjecture, and ontological dispute, punctuated by the procreation of children," and that "the highest accolades should go to the pug and [his] parents, for it makes no sense to praise the fruit and condemn the tree."

A great poet of the following era, Julian Jul, once wrote, "To each his own pug," and these great words have been confirmed by more than one biography.

Helen Hammill was born in a time when the stuffing of pugs was no longer acceptable, in a place where the ripping out of tongues was regarded as "a barbarity equal to impaling on bamboo." In accord with the commendable slogan "Save the Mad," rather than throwing people into dungeons, they were protected in special institutions. And not only Kamadeon, but many other artists as well applauded this humane custom.

Helen Hammill led the way. Let us cast a brief glance into the fate of this uncommon woman, whose medical history began with the words: *coma paradoxalis socialiter fausta*.

If the turning point in Alfred de Verbaal's life was the encounter with the pug, then in Helen Hamill's life it was undeniably Augustyn Hrab who fulfilled the pug function.

"I was awakened one night by a pain in my arm," a thirty-year-old Hammill confessed one autumn in an interview with Sylvia Klosch, writer and wife of the writer Livingstone Mubarak. "I opened my eyes and caught sight of a man who, seeing that I was not sleeping, lightly *jabbed* me in the arm and disappeared. I suddenly understood that we had known each other for centuries."

Two facts cast an interesting light on Hamill's statement: the pain apparently precedes the *jabbing*, while the *jabber, having jabbed*, disappears. What we have here is a case of a breakdown both of causality and of the law of physics that precludes the possibility of dematerialization in broad daylight.

Pir Italy-Loch, Hammill's long-time physician, determined that "All we can conclude is that the man Hammill describes was a dream." Similarly, Arnold Cyryl, the author of the monograph *Dreams: The Terrible Dreams of Helen Hammill*, claimed that "Hrab existed solely in her mind." Noah Jeh, Hammill's husband, went so far as to claim that "Helen merely dreamt of a mosquito, and in her typically female way, she projected its jabbiness onto a man." This thesis was supported in a way by Hammill herself, who in a letter to Hrab confessed, "Darling, I saw a bumble bee in the garden and, led by a prescience that it might be you in a different guise, I was very nice to it."

Helen's other letters to Augustyn provide us with further information. "In the sunless brightness I caught sight of a crow. I recognized him as you, and suddenly it dawned on me that love can assume the form of a bird"; "Whenever I caressed a wall, it was you I was caressing"; "Whenever I ate carp, I had the feeling I was eating our son." Sylvia Klosch adds that in time, "Helen began to sense in all forms the presence of Hrab," and "more and more often she took to kneeling before cows or stroking chairs."

What is immediately striking in all these pronouncements is the almost god-like omnipresence of Hrab. "She felt him inside, too," asserts a childhood friend, Gustav Mobil. This same Gustav, when asked about Hammill's spiritual orientation, is said to have muttered, not without irony: "Pantheism with a tendency toward hierophania." Be that as it may, and leaving open the possibility that, as Cyryl suggests, "Mobil was confusing hierophania with mythomania," it is generally agreed that, "sleep was an overwhelming influence in

[Hammill's] life, and she sank ever deeper into it."

Until she met Hrab, Helen Hammill was a "seemingly naïve, but upon closer inspection, quite cunning little vixen." "Her wrists, like her opinions, were touchingly slender," and "the way she ate ice cream awoke in men not so much desire as a maternal feeling." She laughed often; although, as she herself admitted, her laughter contained "a fair degree of fraud." When deep in one of her reveries, she was, in Gustav Mobil's words, "an inspired plum." By the age of eight she had already read the complete works of Kamadeon; her school essay, "Who Goes, Stays" won first prize in an interscholastic literary competition. Writing, however, held little attraction for her. As Sylvia Klosch says, "Helen was never more than half present, she always seemed to be waiting for something"; while Mubarak, adds that "she very often gave the impression of being unconscious."

Mubarak's observation seems to have been quite apt. Let us compare it to Hammill's account in her novel, *Infinite Delight*, written a year before her death: "As an alternate life, the dream spreads over into reality and leads me down the incomprehensible meanders of forefeeling. Now I know everything, I understand everything, and my imagination is the source of infinite delight. Considering what others call common sense, should I regret having squandered it?"

Hammill was never a defeatist. She liked change, which she saw as "the evolution toward perfection." In her youth she often changed the color of her hair, which, as Cyryl writes, "always went hand in hand with a change of husband." The exact number of Hammill's marriages is not known; if hair color really were any indication, it would have to be around forty. But as it happens, forty is an exaggeration. Gustav Mobil claims she had at most eleven husbands; Noah Jeh says nine; and according to Sylvia Klosch, "Helen [wedded] only once in her life, and on top that, in a veil." Klosch's statement is contradicted by the photograph Jeh identifies as their wedding portrait;

in it Hammill wears a hardhat, not a veil. Arnold Cyryl explains this peculiarity of costume: "As she attached no importance to clothing, Hammill probably went straight from the construction site to the wedding." This last statement requires some elaboration, for it is not true that Helen did not care about clothes. She cared, oh did she care; this is confirmed by those biographers who have counted her sweaters and estimate the number of turtlenecks alone at over a thousand. Furthermore, Cyryl neglects to explain what were Hammill's motives for being at the construction site. Gustav Mobil's view, that "Helen was probably having an affair with an engineer," throws the whole matter into an interesting light. In her last story, "Tools and Turbines," Hammill herself admits that she had been "haunted by engineers [her] whole life," and Sylvia Klosch confirms this by relating a humorous but telling little story: "Helen had a perverse attraction for them [engineers], which in time grew into a terrible obsession. Once, an Ethiopian prince who played the bongos fell in love with her. He was a beautiful man with a noble face and Gothic hands; they made a beautiful couple. On the day he proposed to her, the prince told her that he wanted to go to university. When she asked him what he wanted to study, he answered: mechanical engineering, and Helen fainted."

By no stretch of the imagination was Augustyn Hrab an engineer. From the scant information we have on him we know that "he made no distinction between cement trucks and cranes," that he "mistook jigs for drill bits," and "he always crossed himself before screwing in a light bulb." Besides, he "was a lanky and taciturn man," "elusive as a Chinese shadow." Noah Jeh points out that "he was often in the company of a youth and a donkey," and in his brilliant *Recollections from the Field* Livingston Mubarak describes how "Augustyn would spend hours ogling a windmill and brandishing a stick." We also know that Hrab was a bookseller by trade, that he owned a horse, and that his favorite book was *Sons of the Dungeon* by Alfred de Verbaal.

There is no data to suggest that Hrab was ever attracted to Hammill. As one unconfirmed source states, "[Augustyn] was scared of lewd women, and he avoided the ones who weren't." Nevertheless, it is possible that they did meet. Helen wore over her heart a tooth that she claimed, "fell out of his mouth"; she claimed to have other such relics, although their provenance appears to be rather suspect. Questionable, too, is the authenticity of two letters that, twenty-three years apart, Hrab is said to have written to her. The authorship of these letters is even more difficult to determine because no one has seen them; and in Cyryl's interview with him, all that the putative author would say was "Hmm."

The actual Hrab appears to have had little in common with the Hrab perceived by Hammill. This should not surprise us; she herself admits that she had "always been fascinated by the incomprehensible divergence of perceptions that different people may have of the same thing."

It was to this very divergence that many years earlier the biographer of Putya Zhynikowski was referring when he wrote, "According to everyone there, within half an hour Putya had danced out heaven and all its angels, while by his own account he had fallen to the depths of hell, from where he observed in pain the flat feet and souls of the assembled flatterers." And in his *Autobiography with a Doggy*, Alfred de Verbaal recalls, "When I saw the pug, I felt something painfully sharp pierce my heart. The pain got so unbearable that I fainted. After bringing me round, Aurelia assured me that I had impaled myself on the penknife I was wearing on my chest; but I knew otherwise: it was his glance that had run me through."

Like Alfred de Verbaal, Helen Hammill was considered mad. But madness won't strike the pen from one's hand. To the contrary: her best works were written in half-dream during consecutive stays in mental institutions. She died in an empty room, surrounded by fame.

Invited to her funeral, Augustyn Hrab transformed himself before the eyes of the mourners into a silver birch and confessed: "I have led her up the garden path for the sake of art."

zoom

1.

It was going on four in the morning when Jacob Mushell got up off his mattress, slid his feet into sandals, and brushing crumbs of tobacco from his shorts, made his way to the kitchen. He pulled a beer out of the refrigerator, opened it, and walked to the window.

Outside the window at this hour there should have been bright, flashing neon lights, a string of car lights, a cigarette in the hand of a girl freezing outside the pub, or a star, at least. But no, there wasn't any of that — outside the window was the most ordinary sort of darkness under the sun. The one unbroken streetlamp illuminated a hole in the sidewalk, and nothing shone in the overcast sky except the red halo of the TV tower.

Diligently sleeping off its weekend drunk, the city entered Monday.

"Three minutes more," thought Jacob, squinting at the alarm clock. "And if she hurries, then it'll be twenty minutes. And if she's late? Well, if she's late, then we'll miss it for sure." He sighed and walked away from the window.

"Tell me a goodnight story," he asked, sinking onto the cushion. He nuzzled the leg of the table with his mouth, crushed the beer can, and sobbed. "You know very well words weigh nothing and that I refuse to believe in them. I'm not asking for much, just a little dose would be enough. Just tell me something, before you wake up. That's all I want."

At this hour, bells should have been ringing in the distance, and the silhouettes of slumbering houses should have begun to emerge in the light. But nothing rang, and nothing began to emerge; there were no bells, there were no houses. The night went on undisturbed, like a loneliness swaying in time to the alarm clock's ticking.

Jacob Mushell pressed his back against the carpet, brought the can to his eyes, and read: Tastes Best When Refrigerated.

"My baby," his mother would sigh now, if she only could. "He was always so overdramatic, always so oversensitive; he always went crawling under the table!"

"Iiiiii, Mama," Jacob would squeal in response, disgusted like someone whose childhood memories always bring on a hard-to-define irritation. "Can't you see I've changed! I've been in forty-three countries, slept in countless different beds. I've hung out with people of all walks of life and colors of skin: commanders, warriors, beekeepers, priests, scribes, ping-pong players, gentlemen, lace makers, mediums in trances, and anthropologists — why, once I even brushed a caterpillar off the back of the Queen of Jazz!"

"But all it takes is one little quarter-century, and here you are, back where you started from: Under the table." Mother would gently point out.

"It's not true!" Jacob would shout, blanching in horror. "It's all a matter of language, you see. English makes me reserved, Sanskrit makes me unapproachable, Swahili brings me together with out-of-the-ordinary friends, and German makes my teeth grow huge. It's only when I act like I used to be that I start feeling like crawling under the table. I cry, lose my equilibrium, I fall into a kind of shaking, into something thick and gooey . . ."

"That just means you have a craving for jelly pudding, my prodigal son," his mother would calmly explain. Then she would push a cup of lukewarm, skinned-over milk in front of him, and probing his ear with her finger, whisper: "Sweet potatoes — *feh!*"

Jacob Mushell got up from the floor. He took a long swig of beer, walked to the window, and looked out at the street. From around the corner, a truck appeared.

"If there's a woman sitting behind the wheel, it means there's still hope," he thought and, putting his last egg in the same basket, added: "And if she's Chinese and doesn't have bangs, it means you love me and we'll live happily ever after."

It was going on four in the morning.

2.

Rebecca smiled grimly at her own thoughts. Her insomnia hadn't let up for months, her hands kept shaking, and although the wine kept gushing more and more, life seemed as bleak to her as Venice had to Joseph Brodsky. For when it is observed from the perspective of hunger, abundance becomes a parody of itself, and instead of gratifying, it dumbfounds the viewer with perversely superfluous excess.

The seasons changed; time rushed forward, full of acts that lost all meaning the moment they were completed: Getting out of bed, making the bed, going back to bed. Rebecca's bed, like her life, was a hopelessly empty replica, a Brodskyan Venice in which, however, a gondolier would turn up now and then. He would grunt and sweat, whistle, and hum *o sole mio*, and after crossing to the other bank, invariably vanish through the door of an equally unreal palazzo.

O women, women. Wouldn't it be possible, just once, to be a man about it, about all those things that are greater than the turbulence in the double chamber of one's own congested emotions? War, for example, pestilence, Wittgenstein, or ecology?

"Or monsters," prompted a muffled whisper. "The world is just stuffed with monstrosity."

It was Leonard's whisper. Although Leonard himself was not there, he was represented by his toenail, which was shut inside Rebecca's locket.

"Monstrosity is an important issue," Leonard's toenail assured her. "Look at all the plagues of the world: racism, sexism, colonialism . . . Instead of crushing glasses in your hand, why don't you concentrate on global issues?"

"Because I'm adjacent," Rebecca shrugged her shoulders, crushing a glass in her hand. "I have to watch out I don't get too close."

"To whom?" asked the anxious toenail of Leonard. "To what?"

"To the context," Rebecca groaned, licking up the blood. "For as long as I can remember the context has always eluded me. Whenever I tried getting in somewhere, I would find myself either above, or below; either I was too heavy or too light, too confident or too unsure. I don't know, I never fit in anywhere. So finally I just gave up. And ever since, I've been adjacent, you see, an ideal symbiosis: proximity undisturbed by contact."

Leonard's toenail scratched its head.

"You're not making this all up by any chance, are you?" he grumbled. "Maybe the winter was too long? Maybe you got snowed in, and that's where these stuffy theories are coming from?"

"Maybe," Rebecca agreed. "I haven't spoken in months. Now and then someone tries to cheer me up, or else get on my nerves, or make me fall asleep. But I keep clear of words. Words are only ever knives or bandages, didn't you know?

Leonard's toenail blushed.

"Don't you find this constant inconstancy oppressive?" he said, changing the topic. "Don't you long for something peaceful, permanent?"

"I'm so faithful to you it makes me sick," Rebecca laughed, smoking a cigarette. "Really, I'm not bored at all. I paint various things from memory — sometimes saints, sometimes little ducks, sometimes whores. Have you noticed how hard they are to tell apart?"

Leonard's toenail hung its head.

"Oh you," he whispered. "And I'm the one who was supposed to die, but this time . . ."

"Oh no, not yet," Rebecca interrupted and looked at her watch. She put out the cigarette with her heel and set off in the half-light of the street for home.

It was going on four in the morning.

3.

The silhouettes of slumbering houses began to emerge from the darkness, a cigarette tossed on the sidewalk glowed, the rumble of an engine disturbed the silence. A truck drove down the street. A Japanese woman sitting next to the driver wiped off the mirror, fixed her collar, and disappeared along with the truck around the corner.

And to think that happiness was so close.

Jacob Mushell crushed the beer can, wished himself a happy thirty-fifth birthday, and went back to bed. The stars faded.

After its diligently slept-off weekend drunk, the city entered Monday.

4.

So what to do with them all? If what keeps them apart is what joins them together, they still won't be able to get close to each other.

But they won't be able to get away from each other either.

la mala hora

. . . and he took the nail from his pocket, gouged six little holes into the chestnut; then, tucking matches into the holes, he made the little devil two horns, two legs, and two little hands.

What I'm talking to you about is love.

It was, like now, late November, and I still hadn't completely recuperated from "A Literary Summer" and "Writing in September," when I was invited to attend an "Autumn of Poets." The reason for festivals like these was never clear to me. I don't remember ever striking up a friendship at one, or making an acquaintance that went beyond exchanging addresses. Still, I loved traveling and exchanging addresses, and afterwards coming back with my wallet full of snappy business cards, smiling, feeling reborn, light of step like a happy fellow who, having met one too many writers in his life, had long ago lost his faith in words. But lack of faith needs replenishing, too, so it wasn't long before I booked my ticket to Mala Hora.

It was, as I discovered, a pretty strange place. I wouldn't say it was gloomy, but neither was it terribly pleasant. The "mountain" promised in its name turned out to be not only "little" but practically flat — an insipid mound, on top of which they had built, over the course of several decades, what looked like a barn made of concrete and had christened it the "Palace of Culture." Aside from horse stables, a golf course, and a dubiously picturesque town square — where my hotel, which bore a hallucinatory resemblance to the Palace of Culture and was called for some mysterious reason "Hotel Panda," was located — there wasn't much to speak of in Mala Hora. And yet I remember in perfect detail how one late afternoon as I was walking down a road edged on either side by a row of bare (it was that time of year) chestnut trees, I found myself suddenly overwhelmed with unimaginable emotion. Although I no longer cried as much as I used to, I still could be considered a sentimental person, very sentimental in fact. It was still enough for it simply to rain, or for a rainbow to appear, or snowflakes to fall on my eyelashes, for me to burst into tears. I still had the same smile I'd always had, which women liked to call "boyish." I still wore my mittens attached by a cord through my sleeves. I refused to open a bank account because banks filled me with metaphysical horror. I read Marquez in the bathroom and still found myself jerking off to certain passages in *One Hundred Years of Solitude*. It was the same old me, no doubt about that, but some things had definitely changed. Not that I had grown up, become a man, whatever that was. The phrase "grown man" sounded awful, like "wart" or "hirsute" — it reminded me vaguely of rotten bananas, and even as a child it had filled me with revulsion. Nevertheless, I did feel that I had grown up. I no longer had any problem standing in the longest of lines and filling out paperwork all on my own, or with angelic insincerity patting the head of my cabbage-addicted neighbor's fat kid. I even stopped kicking poodles when no one was looking, and I no longer harassed the cat with the vacuum cleaner, since I had given him away to a friend. I had become, I sensed, a human being, shaken free of many contradictions.

Maybe that was the reason I stopped writing poems? I don't know. Nor do I know which was greater, my loss or my gain. When I met Sara, I stopped looking for an answer. Sara put to sleep inside me most of my other questions, too. This truly remarkable, thirty-eight-year-old girl possessed an amazing gift for making men out of the most recalcitrant little boys. I hung Christmas lights over my bed, I pinned a ladybug to my collar, and drunk with the thought that my luxurious orphanhood had finally come to an end, I scratched into the bedroom door a giant daisy, big as the sun.

"What the fuck, are you nuts?" said Sara.

I fell in love with her at first sight, so I can't tell if she was really beautiful, or only seemed so to me. Either way, she had an unquestionably exceptional neck, almost ostrich-like, though covered not with feathers, but with the pureblooded down of a gypsy queen. Crowning this impressive neck was a nobly egg-shaped head festooned with a helmet of short, dark hair. Sara's nose, another matter entirely, was an intrepidly curved hook, an exact replica of Bob Dylan's. I was charmed as well by the way she walked, the enchanting gait with which she seemed to traverse all life's diagonals. Only the color of her eyes was never clear to me; they were strange eyes, two chameleons, mirrors turned forever inwards.

We met years ago in Port Strawberry, a seaside village I found myself in completely by chance. In those days I lived by working jobs as occasional as they were temporary. I wrote uncompromising poetry and in my contempt of competition dreamed secretly of one day refusing the Nobel Prize. I spent a week in Port Strawberry, in the empty villa of a friend of friends who had to go away suddenly and urgently needed someone to take care of his dog. I agreed without hesitation, especially since the dog was a wolfhound and not a poodle; and even though when I got there it turned out that I'd have to water the plants, I had more than enough time on my hands. I met Sara while walking the dog one evening. She was wearing a backless black dress and walking along hand in hand with a man who gave me the impression of a wilted flower child. He was skinny, wore his buttock-length hair hung in a braid, and his long vest, which looked just like the ones latter-day flower children wear as they parade around India, was embroidered with Sanskrit mantras. Peeking out from under the shirt like the puffy sleeves of a harlequin's blouse appeared two legs in rather loose trousers bound at the ankles with rubber bands. From the very first I was completely revolted by him, and thought to myself that the elegant woman at his side must be madly in love with him not to have gone red with embarrassment. Out of curiosity, just so I could see her face, I let the dog run ahead — and that's when it happened. The dog apparently mistook the man for a bone. Much later, Sara still would laugh whenever she remembered how he danced then, gesticulating wildly with his legs, until finally, after throwing her a glare cut with a fakir's penknife, he ran away and never came back. As it turned out, he wasn't Sara's husband at all, as I originally feared, but a random, run-of-the-mill acquaintance who smoked smelly cigarettes made of leaves bound with twine and wouldn't show his teeth when he smiled, and who after four beers held up his fists to his nose one in front of the other and bellowed, then claimed that he was really the son of Parvati and Shiva, the elephant of wisdom, and that he had been reincarnated in Port Strawberry for the sole purpose of one day meeting a young woman in a black dress who would arrive there on vacation.

"I really never thought he'd be such a wuss," said Sara.

Sara, like everyone for whom making a decision is the greatest of tortures, had a weakness for synthesis, and that was why, although we had been together for five years, we still lived apart. Five years earlier, Sara had taken leave of her good-hearted brother Tiff, a man who won the title to his extraordinary qualities only after they stopped sleeping together. I don't much believe in people's good-heartedness, and not at all in the good-heartedness of big, soft-like-a-teddy-bear brothers like hers, who, when he was jilted by a woman, would devour a whole pot of honey, take a long walk, then go back and give her a whole armful of blue balloons. I never met him in person, but Sara's stories gave me the impression of someone who wasn't so much a saint as a man with a secret all curled up in a little ball inside him. Tiff was an architect; his perfectly round buildings looked remarkably like globes that had wandered out into the street. Sara insisted that things had been different in the beginning, that his early buildings were awfully thin and pale and looked like spears of asparagus and made everyone want to puke, and how it even got to where she could no longer afford facials and had to resort to Nivea instead, and that it was only under her unrelenting influence, year after year, down a path of much renunciation and arduous work, that Tiff was able to bring his aesthetic to a state of perfection. He brought his body to a similar state, as well, and the emblem of this change was that he traded his rickety *i* for a solid *o*, and changed his name from Tiff to Toff. It shouldn't surprise me that after such creatively spent years it was hard for Sara to throw away her own work, and that she simply didn't know, not at all, how to leave Tiff-Toff on his own. She had taken on not only all the responsibility, but the sadness, too, that flowed from his eyes each time she packed her suitcase, along with the guilt, which was greater than I could ever imagine, even though I was the one, the only one, behind it all.

In time I developed as well a feeling of fraternity with Tiff-Toff, and the sadness that flowed from my eyes whenever Sara packed her suitcase led me once, although I was strictly forbidden to do so, almost to call him up. I was sitting next to the telephone and had just finished off the wine, when suddenly the phone started to ring all by itself, and Sara informed me that she wasn't at home, but somewhere else entirely, and that one day she would explain everything. I never did find out where she was that time, just as I never learned where she spent many other evenings, when she would kiss Tiff-Toff on his sad cheek before going out and wish me good night from a payphone.

I tried unsuccessfully to subdue the fear that in this new form crept into my everyday life. Many things frightened me, from the obvious ones, like her empty dresses on my hangers, to the more mysterious, the future, for instance. Sara came twice a month, and deprived of any other order, it seemed as if I began and ended with her visits. Her telephone calls, though rarely comprehensible, filled me with such enormous happiness that I would bring the telephone to bed with me and wait, and unable to wait any longer, at half past whatever cigarette to dawn, I would drop off into uneasy sleep and dream of nothing. Light trickled out of the shadows in a thin stream, and I grew used to waiting as one grows used to semi-darkness. I don't remember if I had any friends then other than my hash dealer and my cat, who I was always harassing with the vacuum cleaner. Even the women I once had written poems for, but who, divested of my imagination, turned out to be fragments of pretty uneven prose, no longer interested me. I began instead warming up to the old ladies I met in the park; they would smile amiably, and, watching me with their half-blind eyes, now and then would stroke my cheeks with their hands. They reminded me of delicately frayed laces, prayers, and the poems I could not write, because by this time I'd stopped writing altogether, even letters. At least I tried to keep reading. I traversed in foreign vessels my own most hidden recesses; I dove down in fanciful analogies and bore Sara over the thresholds of houses more perfectly round than any ball. But you can't stayed holed up in books forever.

"You shake like jelly on a plate," said Sara.

Turning its great circle, time seemed to be a line made up of unrepeatable segments. Events were only apparently finite, and my forehead, which ranged freely to my crown, was a fact as ruthless as the kind of devastation wreaked by habit. I looked in bewilderment on the traces of Sara's omnipresent absence: Dresses, whimsical fashions dangling from hangers like costumes of ages past, rows of hearts and daisies, desperate waiting mindlessly doodled on scraps of paper, a bottle gathering dust under the table. Only the wall over my bed, the sky of my nights, kept shimmering like it used to. More resigned than sad, I slowly opened my eyes to a life that was blinding in its simplicity, and the connections that I once had broken off as unceremoniously as I now was attempting to repair them ushered me into an unwittingly barren world of business and art. Since I was not qualified for any particular career, I took up my friends' suggestions and eventually started a small press. At the beginning its prospects were pretty dismal, but it ate up so much of my time that I remorselessly gave up the cat to better hands and devoted myself entirely to work.

After that, my time passed quickly, although I admit, in spring, things could have been better. Spring played havoc with my composure; it dragged me from the shadows and laid bare the scars that were trying to forget my wounds. Galled by the budding of new foliage, uneasy, I spent the evenings wandering in the park, and like an old man well acquainted with the taste of the ephemeral, I looked compassionately at the birds awhirl in their transitory happiness. I cannot say whether I longed then more for Sara or for autumn to arrive. Captivated by the luminous voice, I sank into darkness, and with the turntable set for continuous play, I stared for hours at the screen of my ceiling.

It was only the summer's languidness that, perversely enough, gave me back my strength. I once again drew open the shades, let a feverish faun into the room, and auguring my end from his temples, threw myself again into a whirlwind of work. Slogging away night after night, I looked for life in the manuscripts strewn about my desk, and though I found nothing, not even death, I looked further. But there were only rows of marionettes stiffening for no one, thoughts born of hands, leaden bubbles blown from straws. But I refused to give up, and sometimes at daybreak as I was cracking open the thousandth shell, I'd come across a sentence that instantly lifted the weight of dejection from my eyelids. It was for mornings such as these that I lived then. Deaf to opinions both whispered and shouted, serving as my own oracle, I still don't know when I earned my reputation for being such an uncompromising publisher, a man people clung to as much as they avoided. It's nothing unusual; those who've learned how to suffer in silence can't help but be annoyed by the noisier declensions of pain. So I mercilessly persecuted poets whose only gift was for rhyming their own frustrations. And the sorrow they wrote down for the sake of profit both stripped them of all honor and filled me with revulsion. I wrote: "Love, for fuck's sake, bawl your eyes out, get a good night's sleep, and *then* start writing." It's true, I was swelling up with my own power. And even though I was smoking more than eating, my body glowed with a healthfulness that stirred others to admiration.

I won't claim to have been well liked, but that wasn't at all what I was after. Occasional flings always struck me as a waste of time; and frankly, as a publisher I could not allow myself the luxury of genuine affection. Whatever that was, it wasn't an option! Even the most innocent friendship with an author had the seed of a misalliance hiding somewhere inside it; fortunately for me, I had no Samaritan tendencies to speak of, and what's more, and above all else, my heart had only one door. At some point Sara had shut that door behind her, on her way out, or maybe on the way in, even I wasn't sure anymore. Her omnipresent absence had turned to air, which I breathed completely naturally and unawares.

I liked literary conferences the same way someone might like the sea. Submerged underwater, laughing, I gathered seashells and algae and put them in a drawer I'll never open again anyway. "Am I still the same person, Sara?" I asked as I took the cards out of my wallet. But my absent one did not have a voice. My absent one, kissing her sad Tiff-Toff on the cheek and wishing me good night from roadside payphones, made men out of the most recalcitrant little brats. Her eyes, directed inwards as they were, expressed an everlasting augury of bliss.

The tenderness that overcame me during that walk down the chestnut-tree-lined road was not so much a new feeling as one that I had long forgotten. I watched the boy who, for whatever reason, picked a chestnut off the ground and in inhaling the November air suddenly tasted the smell of cinnamon and snow. A smell like that, which reminded him not so much of something lost as of something hurled into the abyss of his memory, filled him with an unspeakable aliveness, like the smell of a Christmas tree or of a woman — like love, which is really such a simple thing, after all. And suddenly, because the important things rarely happen any other way, suddenly he felt everything opening up again, and he began to rush, really, to rush, because he finally had stopped being so afraid of everything. He rushed and left everything behind him — absurdity, excess seriousness, the squeamishness, and even, for fuck's sake, vulgarity. He inhaled late autumn, holding it in, and released from his nostrils poems that dissipated the moment they touched paper, and so he hurried to give them titles, so that at least their names would survive. This one should be called such-and-such, he would think to himself and immediately forget it, because he had already gone even further, on to inaugurate thresholds and metaphors, because he had started once again taking pleasure in all these things. And as he went on, at an oblique angle to absurdity, seriousness, squeamishness, and, for fuck's sake, vulgarity, he suddenly understood just how sad he had become lately. And when he finally comprehended this, he found himself standing in the last glimmering light of joy. And suddenly, because the important things rarely happen any other way, he no longer regretted anything, neither himself, nor his love, which now was more than welcome to end, even if it had never really begun. The weight of a thousand-year-old tortoise was lifted from his chest, and his heart beat with gratefulness, and out of his sleeves tiny cold and white sparks flickered endlessly. They settled on the ground and on the crowns of trees and were beautiful like snow.

"I'll make a little devil for you," he decided . . .

waning luster

When the hot sun had finally set, a still-young woman of about thirty went to the windows in the south room of the white villa and drew the blinds. Stefan, the neighborhood voyeur, watching from around the corner, was unfortunately no longer able to see her as she packed her suitcase, stood in front of the mirror, and made faces. He waited a moment longer, withdrew into the depths of the street and vanished, disappointed, into the nearest bar.

The little town sank into dusk. The rain's monotone march was disturbed now and again by the meowing of cats, and the unambiguous groans coming out of half-opened windows mingled with echoes of family arguments and the noise of shattering glass. It was early May — a propitious time for planning changes and for changing plans.

Which is why Bertha had no intention of going to bed. She felt the need for change growing inside her, and although change terrified her more than stasis did, she kept feeling more and more its coming inevitability. Held by her own reflection, she alternately pouted, grinned, pursed her lips, sucked in her cheeks, blew kisses, and coquettishly winking at an upper corner of the mirror, whispered, "Bertha, darling . . ." Startled by her own voice, she started laughing. But it was a laugh that did not portend laughter.

Tired of her own multiformity, Bertha went to a bookshelf containing a single book, and from behind the fat tome, *Dictionnaire de la philosophie*, she pulled out banknotes stashed there for who knows what reason.

The night passed slowly, and her impressions of the preceding day took on increasingly the form of an unavoidable decision.

When the sun rose again, Stefan peeked out as usual from around the corner and was surprised to see the window wide open, but no one in the room.

Every bee has its beginning, and so we'll go back to the stinger, that is, to the day Bertha kissed her husband on the cheek and left for the bakery. Unlike other women, she had no obligations. So she leisurely wandered the lazy streets of Ips, amused herself a moment with a cat, and unconcernedly tossed a coin to a street musician playing a flute before sitting down on a bench awash in the morning sun.

Neither weather nor nature will enter our report. It's enough to mention that in the sky a sparrow was circling and that Bertha's heart was expanding with a strange longing for something not so much great as simply a little different.

"How strange," she thought, observing the stooped-over passers-by. "For generations these people have been mooning down the same paths as ever and none of them has ever thought to turn off somewhere."

In fact, the Ipsians had become a self-contentedly conservative community: They got their water from the faucet, their knowledge from coffee grounds, and only the local newspaper could get them to change their opinions.

Bertha, however, was not a typical Ipsian. She saw too much and knew too little, and what's worse, she was aware of it. And so she emitted with diminishing strength her sparks of joy when she thought of the sun shining as it had for years through six of the twelve windows of her eight-room apartment — an apartment she lived in along with a number of stuffed fish, a pair of disarmingly fat guinea pigs, and a husband.

Fate had been extremely generous to her forty-year-old husband, and not a few Ipsian males, if asked what they most wished to be, would have answered unhesitatingly: Married to Bertha. This was hardly surprising, for not only did Bertha have a fine body, she was not very talkative, a trait that particularly suited her husband, who was a passionate angler. Other than that, he was innately a self-contented sort of idiot and never once called his happiness into question. He most certainly was not one of those men whose thirst for the absolute makes them take off like moths for the sun only to be reduced to ash. No, Bertha's husband's happiness was entirely mundane and not at all difficult to understand.

"And here are our little ones," he would say proudly each time he showed visitors the stuffed fish, by which they were to understand that Bertha had inspired him to catch them.

His collection was housed in two adjoining north rooms and was worth as much as an average husband could earn in half a century, which is why Bertha never lacked for earrings, woven rugs, gilded chamber pots, baroque secretaries, or many other things that husbands employ to mete out their love.

She had forgotten long ago what his name actually was (Dionysus? Charles? Solomon?), so she smiled as sweetly as she could and on Sunday mornings, depending on the season, would put the corresponding concerto of Vivaldi on the stereo for him. Sometimes she even went on her own and bought her husband some little trifle to make him happy: underwear, a fish hook, a fishing rod inlaid with mother-of-pearl, or a ticket to the commercial fish fair. Oh the energy she spent providing proofs of her love, if only to compensate for the painful lack of it!

"And tomorrow we'll go to the carnival!" was how she would promise him good night, and with a wave of her slender hand she would retire, relieved, to her room.

Bertha's silk duvet was full of holes from cigarette ashes. For in the expanses of night, orgies of wind would break out, the air would resound with shrieks, the candle tremble, while with flushed cheeks Bertha engrossed herself in her yellowed copy of Larousse's quarter-century-old *Dictionnaire de la philosophie*.

Sometimes, when she could no longer stand the tension, she

would lay aside the dictionary and take out from her bag a huge stack of magazines.

At this point we must explain that the study of print media was by no means an activity Bertha engaged in out of some commendable need to know the world; no, the press, especially the daily variety, held no interest at all for her. She was just as indifferent to election reports and weather forecasts as she was to accounts of self-immolation among Rajasthani widows or the fashion for diamond-studded belly buttons.

To be honest, Bertha desired not knowledge, but change. But what good is a desire whose object deceives us with countless mirages and like desert air eludes our grasp? Her heart filled with sadness, and this sadness, pervaded with unrest, gave birth to the need for suppression.

It was mainly for this that Bertha leafed through the newspapers.

She indifferently dismissed the sports and politics sections, lingered a moment over the classifieds and the horoscope, and laughed out loud at the crossword puzzle, all in order to throw herself into the unimaginable abysses of the culture pages.

Bertha had other reasons to be interested in this section.

With a trembling hand she smoothed out the crumpled page, wiped her brow, and quickly scanned the bold-faced headlines: "Mona Lisa's Gap-Toothed Smile," "Madame Portnoy Hatches a Complex," "The Clitoris of James Joyce." Such clever metaphors were intended to portray the truth of a literature that, by way of contrast to the *belles-lettres*, was called women's writing; and it was with regard to such writing that a certain Usto had especially distinguished himself, a critic who contended that Sappho, just like Ali Baba and Derrida, was a man.

And then Bertha would clench her little fists.

Although like most Ipsian women she had come to terms with her own nonexistence long ago, Bertha felt in the depths of her soul a rage that confirmed her existence entirely.

"Posers!" she hissed, crumpled up one newspaper after the other, damned the critic Usto to a next incarnation as a Rajasthanian widow, and returned in resignation to the *Dictionnaire de la philosophie*.

At dawn, practically unconscious from stimulation, she turned off the light and fell asleep, still pondering the Epicurean concept of freedom and without even taking her little shoes off first.

But nothing lasts forever.

Sitting on the bench, Bertha fixed her eyes on the musician performing across the street. A rather strange sort of flautist, he wore a loose-fitting, knee-length tunic hanging from his bony shoulders, covering what looked more like a large stick than a body. From under a yellowish cap fused stalks crept down his sunken cheeks, but the whole figure was wreathed in a delicate aureole of red light. Tears trickled from the flautist's unseeing eyes, so Bertha figured that he must be very old and sick with at least twenty illnesses, and this made her sad. But she had to admit that the melody emanating from the flute was exceptionally beautiful and that her sadness, rather than saddening her, filled her with happiness.

She had never felt such a feeling before, which is why it alarmed her so much. So she decided to leave.

When she rose from the curb, the melody suddenly stopped, the musician slumped to the ground, and the flute, freed from his fingers, rolled under the feet of a girl walking by and vanished. The girl halted in her tracks and burst into tears. A woman covered the girl's eyes with her hand, and around the man lying on the ground a group of adults assembled, quick as lightning.

". . . Don't touch him . . ." "infected . . ." "the police . . ."

In these shreds of chaotically shouted sentences a nagging inevitability showed through. Then an ambulance drove up to take the body away, a policeman asked the crowd to disperse, and in a moment life, scrubbed clean of death, again moved in its untroubled rhythm. One detail, however, distinguished this event from other everyday events: When the ambulance drove off, it was empty — the flautist's body had vanished along with his flute.

Standing motionless on the edge of the road, Bertha smiled. She could not help feeling that she still heard the melody and that the melody was wakening in her an atavistic longing for a passion obsolete as the tailbone.

But no matter what happens, it always happens at the right time.

When she got back home, Bertha looked in disgust at the plaque on the door and its carefully inscribed names. She turned the key uncertainly in the lock — the apartment was empty. For a moment she stood in front of the stuffed fish, but suddenly felt her throat constrict and ran quickly to her room. The afternoon sun was shining in the polished surface of the desk, the sleeve of a fur coat was sticking out of the wardrobe, and on the carpet a guinea pig was wrestling with a leaf of lettuce.

It's all so little, she thought to herself, whereas before she had seemed to think it was all so big.

She took her suitcase out of the chest, and as soon as she noticed Stefan's familiar silhouette, she went to the window and drew the blinds.

Night passed slowly.

It was going on four in the morning — the most magical of hours. For it is then that the workers set off for the factory and the unemployed have their revelations. At four in the morning Bertha took out of the drawer a sheet of sand-colored paper, carefully selected a pen of a matching hue, and wrote a letter, not so much to her husband as to herself. This was very likely the first love letter in Bertha's life, and it closed with the heroic word "Farewell!" She put the letter on the refrigerator, caressed the shoes standing in the foyer, and when she jumped off the windowsill, she plunged into the rain-scented air.

A cat meowed, and a sparrow flew from a branch.

farewells to plasma

The Zeroes had one of those marriages that are not so much happy as fated to last. They lived quietly in their houseplant-filled home; since they were childless, they traveled a great deal, and from their trips they brought back souvenirs to inspire further trips: A picture of Mrs. Zero on a suspension bridge, the tooth of a Chinese patriarch, a turquoise talisman shaped like a shinbone, a photo of Mr. Zero in the final stages of dysentery. Yes, the Zeroes very much liked traveling to faraway places. Trips to faraway places, as opposed to places close by, enable distance without at the same time enforcing proximity.

The Zeroes did not own a television. They had once tried owning one — for how can one renounce an evil without first understanding it? And so they came to understand television, and after thinking about it a moment, they first put it away, and then after several weeks, agreeing that both the hours in their day and the thoughts in their heads had increased, gave the television to a distant acquaintance. Of course, in the beginning, the television-less evenings were unbearable: The Zeroes would sit at the kitchen table, apathetically sliding their glasses around. "I saw a Russian today," Mrs. Zero would announce, playing dumb. "He had flat feet and his head was even bigger than yours." "You don't say," said Mr. Zero, becoming unhealthily animated. "And I saw a Korean today: He was skinnier than you and kept discharging green ooze." The word "ooze" sounded monstrous to Mrs. Zero's ears. "You have greasy hair and zits on your forehead," she said, grimacing, venting her disgust. "And you're menopausal!" Mr. Zero cried, stood up from the table, and after tripping over his own shoes, walked in a huff out of the kitchen.

The television's absence dramatically sharpened the tone of familial dialogues and brought to light baser instincts for the now-uncabled couple to indulge in. Not much later, though, Mr. Zero listened to his higher instincts and proudly brought home two computers. The long evenings regained their shaken equilibrium, and the Zeroes' life again moved in its measured rhythm.

Mr. Zero, a portly Pole with the face of a Buddha, was a computer programmer, and a very talented computer programmer at that. He knew everything. The German firm for which he worked was surprisingly appreciative of his intelligence; and although he wasn't after anything, he was promoted from one quarter to the next and was given ever-greater responsibilities to perform. So Mr. Zero started coming home from work ever later. And sometimes it happened that he did not come home at all. Sometimes, for unknown reasons, Mr. Zero would get on his bicycle after work and cruise around the empty streets until dawn, crooning off-key but at the top of his lungs the Polish national anthem, the "Ogiński Polonaise," Christmas carols, and other heart-rending tunes. These were childhood songs, songs of the partisans, battle songs, songs from church. The melodies ran through his memory and flew off toward the placid sky like plumes of smoke and sparks from the campfire in which the national consciousness of the erstwhile Mr. Zero had been formed. But now there was as little left of this consciousness as there was of the campfire itself. This was unfortunate, but what to do? Mr. Zero had lived through plenty of church services and fires, but he had never experienced war, with the possible exception of a massacre of tea planters in West Bengal. Mr. Zero's role in that massacre in West Bengal had been passive, that of an accidental tourist, and he had found the songs of the rebellious peasants charming, although once he got to know the words to them, he speechlessly put away his camera and, in the course of several weeks of drinking wheat beer in the company of Nepali highlanders, forgot the useless songs entirely. Unlike the Bengali melodies, the songs of his childhood were impossible to forget. What was worse, they were the only ones Mr. Zero would have been able to sing were he ever asked to sing a song.

Mrs. Zero was in somewhat better circumstances. She was tone-deaf and unable to sing even scales. She once had paid a great deal for this handicap, when a certain Nadezhda, a music teacher in one of Poland's elementary schools, cracked a violin bow over her head. The erstwhile Mrs. Zero not only did not know how to sing, even worse, she had no idea how to defend herself. So after the incident with the bow, the little girl drowned herself in tears, sat meekly in place until the bell rang, and at recess wrote in her diary: *Now I know where darkness comes from. We went out onto the roof, the shadow of the melancholy wise man looked up at the sky and said: We're in the maw.*

Mrs. Zero's childhood was a strange and by no means easy one. But hardship and strangeness are stimulants for the imagination, which is why since childhood Mrs. Zero had lived in a world of dragons, gnomes, and the shadows of wise men crawling over rooftops. This made her neither sad nor proud, however. Mrs. Zero was good-natured and open, and quietly forgave those crimes whose consequences had cut permanent grooves in her psyche. Those grooves flowed not with tears, but with thinking. *The plasma of sensual experiences: light and the monotonous howling,* she wrote once after coming home from school, and although she had no reason to be happy, she danced and skipped happily around her horror-stricken grandmother.

Good-natured and open, Mrs. Zero nevertheless valued solitude over the company of other people, even as a child. For with people, the farther away they were, the more they made her laugh. And even as a child, Mrs. Zero loved laughing. Somehow this laughter had to be released, so Mrs. Zero very persistently sought out ways to express herself. She wrote diaries and poems, painted her own version of Guernica, and even bought a dulcimer and sheet music. Eyes fixed on the notes, she would play "Kalinka" on the dulcimer and calm down.

As often happens in life, the Zeroes met each other by accident, in Germany, the land of alchemy's eulogists and poetry's hangmen. Mr. Zero was intending to emigrate as soon as possible from there to Canada, Mrs. Zero to Tibet. Until then, she was renting an apartment, and trying, with one arm in a sling, to drive a nail into the wall. This nail was meant to support a shelf for two teacups that Mrs. Zero had been given as a present by a newly married couple overloaded with gifts, and her hand had been put in a cast in the hospital in order to set a finger that she had damaged while cutting onions. Cutting onions paid the rent on Mrs. Zero's apartment. The sensitive Mr. Zero could not stand the sight of a one-armed Mrs. Zero, so he took the hammer from her and began to pound the nail himself. He pounded it in as if in a trance, and after only a few weeks the apartment was filled not only with shelves, but with cupboards, dressers, little tables, and Mr. Zero himself. And on March thirteenth (an impossible-to-forget date) Mr. Zero broke open the plaster cast, massaged Mrs. Zero's hand, and the following day, staggering from lack of sleep, he nailed to the front door of the building a piece of cardboard with his name on it.

Mrs. Zero was not so much happy as content. Now she cut onions only on weekends, she put Tibet out of her mind, and began studying Sanskrit. Mr. Zero, for his part, put Canada out of his mind, and took up pounding nails professionally. In the breaks between pounding nails and massaging Mrs. Zero, he studied computer science. Evenings, the two of them often would get on their bicycle, Mr. Zero pedaling, Mrs. Zero holding her legs in the air, and ride over to the cinema. Sometimes they ran into friends, other times they ran into the police. But they never really wanted to run into anyone, and it was with real relief that they returned to their solitude. In the beginning, they slept together. Mr. Zero, however, snored, and Mrs. Zero always kicked the blankets off him, so they agreed to split the bed and began sleeping on separate mattresses on either side of a wall. After some time, Mr. Zero finished his studies, Mrs. Zero quit cutting onions, and they bought a second bike. Later, they bought a car, took their vacations in Canada and Tibet, and having freed themselves finally of their desires, began leading a normal life. Time flowed like a grass snake forced into a stalk of bamboo.

While Mr. Zero was coming to terms with the computer language Java and singing the "Ogiński Polonaise" at night, Mrs. Zero wrote stories. These stories were very short, void of plot, and, so they said, indigestible. Why, this is merely a sketch for a portrait, the outline of a plot, begging for a crayon to fill it in, a vexing lack of resolution! Mrs. Zero thought that was bullshit. In her opinion, the stories were simply mirrors clad in an iridescent veil, and the critics' indigestion no doubt had something to do with all the pork on the menus back home. Taste can be argued about into infinity, the truth's legs are as short as those of falsehood, and what comes to light always depends on what bag it was kept in before. However it may be, the fact was that no one was reading Mrs. Zero's stories on the train. No one was reading Mrs. Zero's stories at all.

So why did she write? For one, out of worry, for these were not easy times. Like it or not, Mrs. Zero belonged to the generation that came after the generation that everyone had already had enough of. The generation that came after, originally known as the "younger generation," did not age underground; it erupted from the pavement like a geyser of new wine and overnight washed out the palette that had been set carefully by a decade of associations. It wasn't that the straw in their shoes or on the thatched roofs of their barns back home had been set on fire. Straw for them meant straws for sipping drinks in bars in London, Vancouver, or New York. Honor and *patria* were slipped the tongue by a cosmopolitan devil, and the image of God, shattered into a thousand pieces, now took to reflecting at the most unlikely angles like an omnipresent mirror. For the interests of the younger generation were dramatically opposed to those of their own too-rich tradition. The younger generation began to emigrate, and not just internally or for the sake of Western academics enamored of Eastern dissidents. Reassessing their ambitions and peeling onions in Greek restaurants, the younger generation cast itself into a whirlpool of completely different experiences. The prince's twin had simplified a method for begging, and a green light rippled and swelled under his feet like a red carpet.

"Evolution, revolution, or pollution?" Mrs. Zero wrote on the door of the bathroom stall, washed her hands, and returned to the table expertly swiveling her hips. At the table, a redheaded man blowing smoke rings was waiting. This man was not Mr. Zero. While Mrs. Zero was practicing "Kalinka" on the dulcimer, this man had been eating French-fries and ketchup; then, on his three-wheeler, he raced the waves across the Atlantic. Here, however, is where the story ends, since Mrs. Zero still does not know how it continues.

a wonderful day in may

Blue expanse over the roofs, birds waking the sun, petals in the park still untrampled by feet hurrying to work. Really, few things are more beautiful than a Thursday morning in May. And few things are more beautiful than a Thursday afternoon . . . Free of the sanctity of Sunday, free of the routine of taking walks and the smells of dinners, Thursday's sun-filled afternoon pulses with the silence of old ladies, the far-off music of drills, and the lazy chatter of the unemployed.

It was on just such a wonderful Thursday in May that Amanda Świerszcz, whose name was difficult for Bill Though, whose name was difficult for Amanda, got out of bed before the alarm clock, which was set for nine, went off. What woke her was a loud boom and a gurgling, a dream not so much frightening as incomprehensible, which she anyway forgot the moment she woke. So Amanda cheerfully washed her face and brushed her teeth, put on a blue dress, and as her vision brushed against a spider spinning a thread, she sank into a morning reverie. For early morning is when the mind generates its most interesting thoughts, as every artist knows.

Amanda Świerszcz was an artist's wife, which is itself no less an art. She worked for a newspaper, writing horoscopes; sometimes she composed crossword puzzles, too, and as the occasion arose, tracked down missing cats. The reward for the cats was never much, but together with her other income, it made her life more comfortable. All the more because Bill Though could not stand the word "money." Not that he was a do-nothing. No, he was simply a poet, and while he worked hard, he generally did so for free. For this, Amanda adored Bill more than life itself, and this love, which transported her to the heights of invention, allowed her to find pearls even in empty shells.

Bill had just flown over the ocean to read his poems to a group of poetry-enthused millionairesses.

"Say 'Świerszcz'," yelled Amanda coquettishly, waving her handkerchief out the window.

"But first, you say 'Though'," Bill shouted and vanished into the taxi that was taking him to the airport.

It was Wednesday.

On Thursday she woke with a smile on her face. It was May, the pigeons were cooing rhythmically, and as she looked out at the clear sky, Amanda Świerszcz brimmed over with a feeling of early-morning freshness. She ate a soft-boiled egg, wrote an unusually cheerful horoscope for Pisces, and as she sniffed Bill's pajamas, she luxuriated in her own happiness. Darling, I'll track down all the missing cats in the world, I'll compose a crossword puzzle two pages long, and when you get back we'll buy you an everlasting fountain pen, she dreamed, and the wind danced in the green leaves, and the sun, wandering toward its zenith, delicately caressed the faces of the elderly and the unemployed.

May that Thursday last into infinity. And may a happy Amanda dance in her May dress and never find out that what woke her just before nine that morning was the gurgling of an airplane sinking in the ocean.

respite

The greater the lamas are, the lonelier they are.

"Sentient beings are mostly idiots," confessed Lama Diamond Patience into the ragged ear of his only confidante, his faithful nanny goat. "And the masters are greedy do-nothings who live off the handiwork of sentient beings."

The Lama was a master; he knew what he was talking about.

"I have a little story for you," he said and began to laugh.

Nothing could lull the insomniac nanny goat to sleep like Lama's little stories.

"There once was a sentient being of the Theodore variety. Since he lacked other interests, Theodore concentrated on the question of his own identity. He would ask: Who am I, and what consequences does this have?"

"Was he a master?" speculated the nanny goat, being polite; she had no interest at all in Theodore, but she did want Lama to keep talking.

"No," said Lama, shaking his head. "Theodore was a greedy do-nothing."

"Aha," the nanny goat commiserated. "And what consequences did that have?"

Knowing that a captious question deserves an equally captious answer, Diamond Patience slapped the nanny goat on the rump and declared: "The consequence, you little smarty-pants, was an identity."

After such a perfidious riposte the nanny goat had no further questions, so the Lama paused a moment then continued the narrative from the opposite direction.

"For days Theodore would just lie there on his mattress. See, this is how he would lie on it," Lama said as he lay down on the grass and stretched out his arms. It looked exactly as if he wanted to make an angel, more or less like how we all used to make angels in the snow.

"That's how Theodore would lie on the mattress," he said again in disgust. He sat up and added: "Our entire pantheon was utterly repelled, even the bodhisattva Loving Eyes refused to look at the sight, and he broke into a thousand pieces out of distress."

Here Lama wanted to demonstrate Loving Eyes' break-up, but the nanny goat woke up in a fright, covered her ears, and shouted:

"I know, I know, once, when I was teasing my billy goat, I practically broke in two myself, oh did that ever smart!"

"Then just imagine, he smarted five hundred times more strongly," Lama said coolly. "And he wasn't even teasing a goat, he broke up simply out of love."

The nanny goat understood what he was getting at and pulled in her tail. Diamond Patience paused a moment, then continued:

"So we had to act. I made my way to White Lake, asked the pertinent agents for signs, and that very same day a wave cast onto the shore an enormous syllable MA. When a short time later I had a dream about a tortoise, I knew for sure we would have to send Maya to Ips. And that is what we did. With all her experience, Maya took one look at the wrinkles in Theodore's face and discerned a rendezvous, and this, heh heh, with a woman who, though she still knew nothing about it, would soon begin behaving strangely and leave her husband all because of him."

"Leave her husband!" exclaimed the nanny goat, who was a simple creature, raised on the common knowledge that wives are the ones who get abandoned.

Diamond Patience looked poignantly at the goat and stopped talking, just in case. Not for nothing after all was he a lama, and he knew full well that everything is possible, that even a goat's nagging might not drown out that melody that draws women away from their wonted ways.

"It's not easy," he sighed. "The dice have been thrown, and I'll see personally to clearing the field. Just between you and me, even I don't know what will come of it; why, sometimes seeds, once sown, produce completely unexpected fruit."

Seeing that the nanny goat had begun snoring, Lama stopped talking, threw a linen blanket over the creature, stretched his legs, and went out before the building.

In the sky, the moon was shining. As he looked at the moon, Lama uttered the hundred and eight warm wishes, and murmuring a certain very secret mantra, set off on a walk to Mount Kailas.

catharsis

That day as usual at nine o'clock the literary cream of the whole city gathered in an apartment that had been vacated for the holidays. The host's absence didn't upset anyone, to be honest, if only for the simple reason that no one noticed he was gone.

The dining room, which was just as unfurnished for dining as it was for sitting, was packed with men with three-day-old beards, men with fourteen-day-old beards, and smoke. The smoke made one's eyes water, and the men, though their appearance might have suggested something else entirely, were there to manage the fortunes of literature. There were a few girls in the room, too, not many it's true, two, maybe three — but it's rude to count. The girls, dispersed between ashtrays, gazed at the men in mute devotion. Aside from that, they smelled nice, and piping up now and then in admiration, they justified the marvel of their presence.

It was long past midnight when the playwright Pepe Pelz, who was sitting on a lotus, ended his several-hours-long monologue on generic extinction.

". . . poetry, dolphins, prose, even koalas!" he brayed in agony, waking the poet Oval, who was curled up on the windowsill.

There was a momentary consternation on the windowsill.

"I have nothing to do with koalas," mumbled Oval, crumpling his cheeks in his hands.

"But koalae eat eucalypti," said the underrated poet Krzysztof Anna Fluff, showing off his erudition. "Were we to cease sucking cough drops, the demand for eucalyptus would fall and the government of Australia would leave the koalae alone."

"If I stop sucking, I'll have to smoke more," grumbled the writer Bluish. "And whenever I smoke my brand (I can't concentrate on any of the others!), I'm supporting the Ku Klux Klan!"

"So smoke weed!" came a poorly soundproofed croak out of the bathroom; it was Pima di Pasta, author of the well-known column "The Editor Talks Back," which he wrote under the pseudonym of Noodle.

"Even better, smoke what you write," snapped a certain Hoop-Rosemary, an incorruptible critic with a sharp mind and a long lifeline.

As usual, Hoop-Rosemary had gone too far, and with that witnessed two of the girls begin giggling and rush into the kitchen. Chaos broke out in the room.

"Down with the critic!" someone yelled, then someone else echoed it, and in moments a dozen unhealthily hoarse voices took to proclaiming the so-called slogans of the revolution.

"Down with the koalas!"

"Down with literature!"

"Down with everything!"

"That's right, down with the down-withs!" added a tenor voice, rumbling to everyone's astonishment from the carpet. This tenor, as would soon become clear, belonged to the non-smoking, non-chewing, and non-writing writer Bubin Mufka.

"We'll put an end to sucking, an end to smoking, and an end to writing!" shouted the otherwise soft-spoken Mufka. He crawled across the carpet, and began waving his belt around while screaming his head off: "It's the big species that die off first, look at the dinosaur and the novel! The ones most likely to survive are bacteria and haiku! Gentlemen, I propose a minimalism degree zero!"

Though it wasn't the first, it had been a long time since the house had experienced a commotion like this. So it is not strange that no one noticed the shadow that noiselessly detached itself from the wall, slipped in among the postulating literati, and began to extinguish one by one the saucer-bound candles. For a moment all was dark; the shadow crouched in a corner of the room and froze, waiting.

The first to notice the darkness was the sharp-eyed poet Oval. Oval jumped off the windowsill, stumbled into a somewhat disoriented Hoop-Rosemary, and fell under the legs of the shadow.

"A moment ago I could see, and now it's dark!" he yelled. "Who blew out the candles?"

The situation took on definition, while the question of its causal agent rolled around in the silence like a ball of lightning and neutralized the tension that had been accumulating under the ceiling.

"Jesus, it could have been a dragon," said Bubin Mufka, cheering up suddenly. He'd recently seen a film about Hong Kong and knew that dragons could do things like that.

"There's no such thing as dragons," the writer Bluish informed him. "Dragons are hashish for the masses; as far as their existence is concerned, it hasn't been proven."

"You don't exist," said Mufka, getting upset. "Maybe that was a dragon just now, proving its existence all on its own!"

"How do you know it wasn't the ghost of Che Guevara?" Bluish shrugged his shoulders, closed his eyes, and fell to thinking: "Or the ghost of Robespierre, or Montesquieu's ghost, or Cromwell's . . .?"

"Or Kafka's, or Hedayat's," Krzysztof Anna Fluff suggested timidly.

"Or Cavafy's," whispered Oval.

"Or Hephaistos's," declared one of the girls.

The room again fell into a tense silence.

"In my opinion, almost all of you are right," Hoop-Rosemary declared in a slow but audible voice, picked his nose, and since it was dark, quickly ate the booger. "In my opinion," he continued, "the afflicted figure that appeared before us was the spirit of an epoch that . . ."

Here Hoop-Rosemary paused, for the room lit up suddenly and

before everyone's eyes Pimo di Pasta appeared with a lighter in hand.

"Hey guys," di Pasta whispered and with a trembling finger pointed to the corner. "Do ghosts cast shadows?"

Everyone's eyes turned as if on command to the wall at the bottom of which the shadow was crouching. The shadow smiled somewhat uncomfortably and said: "Ladies, gentlemen, please excuse me; I'm here from the administration."

The word "administration" could bode only ill. So Hoop-Rosemary fled that much faster into the bathroom, faster than Oval at any rate, who now was standing in the doorway, ashamed, nervously shuffling his feet. The others all were chewing their fingernails in silence.

"Excuse me," the writer Bluish piped up after a moment, "may we perhaps be told who's casting you?"

"But of course," said the shadow, laughing. He stood and with his head bowed explained: "I'm being cast by a certain monk who due to his advanced age was not able himself to honor you with his presence."

"He's casting you from a distance?" a fascinated Bubin Mufka cried. "Not from Hong Kong, by any chance?"

"Not exactly," sighed the shadow. "I've been cast with a concrete goal in mind, to which, if you'll allow, I'll say a few words . . ."

At this point the writer Bluish sprang from the floor, ran to the wall, and stabbed the shadow in the shoulder with a pen. The pen broke against the wall, Bluish fainted, but the shadow sadly shook his head.

"Unfortunate beings," he said quietly, "I was not sent here as a missionary, and so I'll not impart to you any profounder teachings on the nature of matter. My only purpose, if you'll allow, is to rid this apartment of troublesome demons."

The shadow's voice was warm and resolute, but the literati, once they heard the word "demon," all stood up at once and moved to the door.

"Bluish, that means you, too," the shadow sighed, and with a delicate puff of breath revived the unconscious writer. "I'll count to seven, and you'll disappear with the rest!"

And only a moment later, no one was left in the apartment. The shadow turned on the light, shook his head, and energetically set about emptying the ashtrays.

marchand

William B. Crosswoolf, even in his first year of gymnasium, as a schoolboy with an unusually mature tendency to masochism, avoided T-shirts and shorts like the plague, and even in the hottest of heat waves crammed into one of his tight-fitting sport coats and tightened nooses of silk ties around his neck. His stubbornness in doing this excluded him not only from playing ball, but as well from many other, equally important things, like crawling under fences or groping girls lured into the bushes. But he did not particularly care. Because the only thing that gave him any relief from his quivering adolescence was neither crawling nor groping, but the clandestine expeditions he took to the National Bank. Without understanding why, he loved the dignified odor of the share prices posted inside the vitrines; he would feast his eyes on the sight of mosaic-covered walls, and just pacing soundlessly across the bank's parquet floor made him shudder with bliss. Figuring that he had lost his father, the employees came out from behind their desks and took him by the hand into the storeroom. "Where's your daddy?" they asked. "Dead," Crosswoolf answered truthfully and, undaunted by their bewildered looks, explained: "I came here on my own. It's because everything is so well organized here." At first they thought he was lying, and once they even called the school, but in time they grew accustomed to seeing the boy in the tie; they even came to consider him a sort of mascot, and would proudly inform clients: "He may be little, but he sure knows where to invest." These words, however, were as far from the truth as the comment that many years later the dean would utter in handing Crosswoolf his philosophy diploma: "You're an equation with only one known variable — an immunity to metaphysics." For there was only one truth, and that was the fact that Crosswoolf was becoming infinitely more solitary, and the awkward air he had of a loner, reinforced by the equally awkward legend that he had no penis, led the first woman he ever almost slept with to admit to him, once he had taken off all his clothes, that she was doing it on a dare.

It should come as no surprise then, that in spite of his twenty-seven years, William B. Crosswoolf did not tote his dreams around in a brightly colored knapsack, but in a calfskin toiletry case with brass ligatures on the corners. Fortunately, at this age it was no longer considered so unusual to have a penchant for neckwear, with the possible exception, of course, of bandannas, which at the time were so fashionable among painters, who were, however, about as much of interest to Crosswoolf as the art world itself, which is to say, not in the least. And that is how things might have remained forever, were it not for a certain Monday.

With eighteen months as editor-in-chief of the monthly magazine *Scenes Behind the Scenes* behind him, William B. Crosswoolf rarely had time for breakfast, unless "breakfast" was a raisin bun nibbled while rushing to work, or a handful of the green Koala-brand mints he always ate, which were so intensely odorous the hall would smell like a forest of eucalyptus trees long after he had walked in, and only the people who did not work there ever believed any of Miss Pinzgauer's cover-ups.

There were always more occasions for these cover-ups on Mondays than on any other day, because that is usually when the freelance writers, or "weekend informants," as the staff called them, would drop by. It was hardly fair to call them that, considering that while everyone was equally busy reporting, the freelancers did it on commission while staff members got a salary. What is more, the freelancers were hired to sniff out stories that the staff all too often turned up their noses at, and sometimes this nosing around had to be done after hours or on holidays.

"He hasn't come in yet," Miss Pinzgauer would expertly eye and size up each newcomer, and once she had made sure that this one definitely wasn't staff, she would sigh philosophically: "Really, what do you think telephones were invented for?" On Fridays, as a joke, she would say: "Really, I think you should call again tomorrow," or, if she were in an exceptional frame of mind: "And really, would you please stop scuffing the floor when you walk, you'll wake up the silence!"

Miss Pinzgauer (why not just come out with it) protected her boss not just out of duty, but more than anything, out of her boundless love for him, which suffused the afternoon of her passionless life with the green fragrance of peppermint. She was the world's most loyal secretary, and although effusiveness hardly comes easily to someone as hard-shelled as he was, Crosswoolf had twice given her a raise, and once, ignoring all the smirks, he even invited her to the cafeteria for lunch and for forty-five minutes permitted her to gorge her ears on his inscrutable silence. For her part, Miss Pinzgauer swore to herself her lifelong devotion to him and faithfully kept this oath.

Although it was more than a week until the first day of autumn, the second Monday in September was golden-hued, wet, and so melancholy that as he was tying his necktie William B. Crosswoolf could barely resist tightening the noose for the final time around the neck of William B. Crosswoolf. After all, it would be murder: For when he looked into the mirror, Crosswoolf saw not himself, but someone who for a quarter century was as alien to him as he was despised, and who he already would have done in many times over were it not for his fear of the death penalty. This fear was not ungrounded, and it all had begun with the article.

"A murder in retaliation for a murder is the only kind of murder that is not murder, and that is why it ought to be committed in the name of justice," he had once declared in a hastily written editorial on the death penalty, although this was less his own considered viewpoint than the effect of the full moon and a morning delirium following a sleepless night. The sharp objections from judges surprised him to no end, so he read through his statement carefully, and suddenly, as he was reading through it carefully again, he was reminded of something that for ages had lain timidly nameless in the depths of his memory. Quelling his apprehension, he immediately grabbed a pen, and his next article, written with the passion of a famished adjutant stork, began with these words: "All those fairytales about childhood trauma, temporary insanity, and trances are the direct effects of unemployment among bored psychiatrists." As soon as this second article appeared, matters began moving along at lightning speed. *Scenes Behind the Scenes*, which until then had concerned itself exclusively with noble-minded exposés of tax fraud, revamped its profile, and with its sudden metamorphosis into a voice for radical solutions, it soon had the highest circulation of any women's weekly. And even though Crosswoolf lost the case brought against him by four different agencies and the Board of Physicians, he barely had time to read all the letters from admiring readers. There were so many letters that on this second Monday in September, half because she wished to save him time, and half from her own delight in committing good deeds, Miss Pinzgauer had culled from the letters those sentences that rhymed most nearly with one another, transcribed them in green ink on a piece of cardboard, drew a ladybug on one corner, and pinned the whole thing to the bulletin board:

> *That's right, Mr. Editor! Tear 'em apart!*
> *Up on the scaffold! Rip out his heart!*
> *The editors should see to it they all hang in public!*
> *Why doesn't he cure himself, if he's so sick!*
> *The guy commits murder, and now he's living off our taxes!*
> *Bring back the guillotine! Bring back the axes!*

William B. Crosswoolf acted as if he did not notice the poem, and with a terse "No calls before noon" he disappeared into his office, leaving Miss Pinzgauer in a heaven of menthol bliss. His aversion to her was practically innate. He was repelled by her desperate loneliness, the crude grace of her unfulfilled youth, her sad paunch and padded breasts, and her head, like the head of a stick doll, stuck pathetically atop spurned treasures. Her very existence offended him, which is why he had invited her to the cafeteria that time, intending once and for all to free himself from the warped mirror she was for him. Miss Pinzgauer, I'm dismissing you for no reason at all, is what he thought of saying but said nothing, and as he gazed at her starched collar, he became more and more afraid, because although he knew almost nothing about her, what he did know was not enough not to be afraid.

He had just finished looking through the files on the infamous acquittal of Patz-Oller. This was a case so deadly serious that he had instructed no less than four freelancers and one staff writer to investigate it, and suppressing his impatience at having to wait, he propped his feet on the desk and departed for the soothing land of mosaics and clear surfaces, for the duchy of numerals and relentless symmetries that neither desires nor wind nor thoughts could disturb. The image of the bank that was stored in his memory was his fondest recollection, and it had the same effect on him that a view of the ocean or a forest glade might have on other people. Just before twelve he was jerked out of this state of blissful relaxation by a brutal knocking on his door and the voice of Miss Pinzgauer: "Mr. William, he's here!" Crosswoolf hated it when she called him by his first name. "Enter," he said coldly, and descending prematurely back to Earth greeted the freelancer without smiling.

"Well?" he asked brusquely, gesturing to the chair.

"All the evidence suggests that he was in a kind of trance when he did it," the freelancer said slowly as he sat down and pulled a packet of crumpled envelopes out of his briefcase. "The letters to his mother read like a tragic drama, but his intuition, which on the critical day became a certainty, robbed him not only of control over his own actions, but of his reason as well. Pure and simple, Patz-Oller was possessed by the absolute certainty that . . ."

"From what I know, the man was an orphan," Crosswoolf interrupted him, rubbing his eyes, and once he was awake for good, he blasted the freelancer with every ounce of his heart's accumulated vitriol. "You can go and tell your stories about drama to theater students. And what is this about possession? Was he some kind of Satanist?"

"No, he was an atheist. Maybe if he had believed even in the devil, the tragedy wouldn't have had to happen. But listen, Boss: Patz-Oller believed only in himself and in his own delusions of power, which unfortunately he didn't know how to control. So he began to be afraid, not of the devil, but of something far more sinister: Himself. A series of unfortunate accidents only confirmed this fear, and so he had to destroy what he saw as the dark side of his personality . . ."

"I'm not paying you to psychoanalyze him!" Crosswoolf bellowed. "Are you infected with idiocy? Patz-Oller was just a run-of-the-mill literary hack who got paid pretty well to entertain half a million idiots with his lies! There's the metaphysics for you! I don't doubt that it was frustrating for him, and I'm all for his admitting it. But for God's sake, that's surely no reason to throw people out of windows!"

The freelancer grinned like a fool.

"It's not that simple, Boss," he mumbled, rummaging through the envelopes. "When I was reading these letters, I got the feeling that after Vanessa died his mind started doing some strange things."

"Vanessa?"

"The actress. She wasn't old at all, thirty-something, in perfect health, and pretty. But then the paparazzi delivered this photo of her without any makeup on, and Patz-Oller put it in the gossip section with the caption: 'Vanessa Ray bravely battles lung cancer'."

"What's so strange about that? He was just doing his job."

"Yes, except a short while later she actually did die of lung cancer. At that point he still thought it was just a coincidence. After all, as he said in a letter to his mother, cancer is quite a common cause of death. But then, not long afterwards, the same thing happened again with a certain millionaire, who went up in flames only a week after Patz-Oller had him dying in a burning car . . . Unfortunately, this was only the beginning of a series of deaths that took place exactly the way he described them beforehand."

"Which proves, I gather, that he enjoyed playing God. Great! If I follow you correctly, Patz-Oller nevertheless decided one morning that he'd had enough of his powers and that he could use a death he wasn't able to foresee. So he grabs some random co-worker and: Whoops! Out you go . . .! Of course, since he was an orphan, he had every right to do it, since in a way he'd been thrown out on the street once, too . . ."

"You're mistaken, Boss. He wasn't afraid, he was absolutely terrified. You have to realize, it wasn't just people's deaths he was predicting, but everything: betrayals, kidnappings, divorces, natural disasters. So he started writing about marriages and recoveries from illnesses instead, but who wants to hear good news? All his pieces were rejected, so since he had to do something, he asked to be transferred to crossword puzzles. But his request was denied because they were afraid the solutions would start coming in before the issue had gone to press. So he continued to write, but more cautiously — no deaths, no catastrophes, at most a practical joke in a bathroom somewhere or someone fainting on stage. It goes without saying, these new stories were nothing to write home about, and the circulation began to drop. Basically they were keeping him on only until he'd trained his replacement. They'd already found a replacement."

"Who, the guy?"

"Yes, the one. An ambitious fellow with a vulgar sense of humor and a talent for bullshitting, but with a really big heart. In a letter to his mother, Patz-Oller refers to him as a true son of hers, and I suspect he felt a personal bond with him, something like love, but don't misunderstand me, Boss, I don't think it was an erotic attraction, at least as far as being attracted to yourself doesn't count as erotic. Patz-Oller saw, or maybe he foresaw, a force in him, which he only alluded to in his letters to his mother, and I can completely understand his wanting to be indirect, given the power of the written word... In any case, he was afraid for the guy, as if he had glimpsed some horrible end for him. On the critical day, they were both sitting at the desk, and Patz-Oller was explaining to him techniques for pulling the reader into the story. Then he laid out a series of photographs of a high-ranking politician in a sauna, and told him to come up with a caption. I can only imagine what the caption said. In any case, after he read it, Patz-Oller jumped out of his chair, dragged the fellow to the window, shouted, 'Look, a word's coming down!' before grabbing him by the legs and shoving him out. At the deposition, he confessed that he'd wanted to destroy the evil seed before it sprouted, but later he claimed that he'd wanted to destroy himself."

"Himself? So why didn't he throw himself out the window?"

"In a certain sense, he did, Boss. The other guy embodied the same darkness that Patz-Oller recognized as his own, so by saving him in this way from his destiny, Patz-Oller simultaneously destroyed his own dark side."

William B. Crosswoolf pulled his feet off the desk, walked over to the cabinet, and as he gazed at his reflection in the veneer, said: "Phantasmagoria."

But that is not all he was thinking. To be honest, the whole Patz-Oller affair had at some point ceased to hold any interest for him, and now the only thought on his mind was how quickly he could get rid of the freelancer. So he nodded, acted pensive, said, "In any case, I thank you, Sir," and cast a meaningful glance at the door.

It was all a bad dream, the freelancers were a bad dream, and the staff, and the office, and his tie, and *Scenes Behind the Scenes*, and autumn, which was only ten days away. But the worst dream of all was Miss Pinzgauer. The thought of Miss Pinzgauer was not only a bad dream, but a bad reality, too, and William B. Crosswoolf suddenly felt like a Bill, stranded all alone in the universe. Boys don't like to be spied on, so when he sensed an eye pressed against the other side of the key hole, he rushed to the door, opened it with a vigorous yank, and found himself standing face to face with a blushing Miss Pinzgauer.

"Oh, please come in, I've been expecting you," he hissed, hustling her into the room, then shut the door and locked it. "We certainly have a lot to talk about, don't we?"

He prodded her toward the window and kept talking.

"So you're in love with poor Bill, are you? Everyone loves himself. And you have no one, I completely understand, there are some people for whom a mirror is enough. It's just that I can't stand this mirroring! Stop trembling like that: those who tremble don't deserve love. Weakness should be covered up, but you never even learned how to do that. Look at yourself — it's all there on the surface! It's not my fault you're so pathetic and that you've been wearing that same starched collar ever since you were a child and that the only man who ever took your clothes off did it only to see whether or not you really padded your bra."

The words brought him relief, so he kept talking, and with every word he freed himself further from the dream that he had dreamed so long he'd become thick-skinned as a tank. When Miss Pinzgauer's inert body slumped to the floor, Crosswoolf removed his tie, unbuttoned his shirt, and feeling light and carefree as never before, called the police.

"Sonofabitch, did they ever do her in," the young policewoman blurted out.

"It was suicide," he said quietly, and with the finger marks on his neck safely covered with a scarf, he found himself seized for the first time in his life with the desire to buy a painting.

dog

Clouds were blocking the sun, and Denisa, who was strolling along with all the grace of an open wound, picked up a stick off the ground and threw it as far as her strength would allow. The stick landed three meters away, and Vaclav Dragon, an enormous dog with a good head on its shoulders, looked on, disappointed, howled and bounded off in pursuit of something less attainable. He ended up catching the behind of one of the bitches that had been flirting with him, and Denisa, after first letting out a squeal of horror, rushed over to the catastrophe. "Vaclav! Yuck!" she cursed, jumping over a puddle. "Behave like a gentleman!" The bitch's owner came over in a fury from the other side, and soon the two of them, brandishing leashes and closing in on the humping dogs, were appealing in unison to Jesus and Mary for help. But the holy ones had gone deaf, and it was only Denisa's heroic effort, which consisted in seizing the violator by the muzzle, that ended the fun at its apogee. The bitch was lured away with a rubber bone, and a furious Vaclav, yelping at the top of his lungs, bit Denisa in the calf.

It was, as Ignacy would assert later in conversation with Klara, an expression of doggy frustration at the lack of warmth at home. As it happens, however, Vaclav Dragon, though well loved by many, especially by the waitresses and bartenders, did not have a home. A puppy so sweet you could just eat him up, he belonged for some time to a family and its child, and maybe it was then that he believed in something that he would have to lose: he believed in the constancy of feeling. One day the family moved to another city; and as Vaclav was still growing, always eating, and like any ward could hardly be called overcautious, they had no qualms in handing him off to Ignacy for a while; in fact, they were secretly glad. At first, Ignacy refused, but he loved dogs in his own reason-defying, dogged way, and the ties that bound him to Vaclav Dragon were, he claimed, exceptionally strong. Besides, he was the type of person to live alone, and the temptation of taking walks with a leash, which would make the silence a little less pregnant, tipped the scale in favor of his risky decision. For Ignacy was only too aware that a dog comprises a link of its own in the transactions of human friendships. And although the pleasures of new experiences can wash away the pain of memories, he would never ever forget a certain bitch he'd had for two years of his doggy life and in whom he had died for ages, before being resurrected in Klara's early morning smile.

Until Vaclav Dragon moved into his two-room apartment on the fourth floor of an old apartment house, which had neither wardrobe nor refrigerator, but for that was furnished with affection germinating like new seeds under old snow, until then, Ignacy had truly lived all alone. He avoided women and dogs like the plague, and though he didn't always manage to rein in his sexual urges, he was more inclined to pay for love than to seek it out in furtive glances exchanged on paths through public parks. Besides, no matter if he was deceiving himself, Ignacy had actually fallen in love. It was an entirely new feeling for him this time, love minus the dog, love stripped of all pretexts for encounters, freefalling into the precipitous waters of uncertainty. Ignacy, though bursting with happiness, wasn't entirely sure how to find his bearings in this strange situation. Besides, he suddenly had a lot of time on his hands — suspiciously long mornings, the eternal hours of evenings, everlasting Saturdays and Sundays. Even his visits to coffeehouses had lost their old charm, and that was mainly because when he sat at a table without the dog, Ignacy was in the waitresses' eyes just one of the dozens of other equally dull patrons. Discouraged, he stopped going out and spent his time at home, which like a shell was filled with the sound of the ocean, and like a shell was empty. Soon afterwards Ignacy discovered the virtues of radio, which from then on he had on all the time; and once a month, suffering insomnia from the full moon, he would get out of bed at night, walk to the window, and let go the tears that had been collecting since the dawn of time. On these same nights, he also invariably would have this one particular dream. The dream was always the same: Ignacy is walking the dog, and on a street corner, as if nothing had happened, he runs into Klara.

As soon as Vaclav Dragon moved into the studio with its germinating, snow-covered affection, Ignacy's daily life began by force of circumstance to undergo a transformation. Time contracted into proportion with the silence, and who knows when the radio went mute. Even the waitresses, overcome with desire to stroke the dog's muzzle, took to vying with one another for opportunities to stop by the coveted table. Above their sniffed skirts their abashed eyes would sparkle, and these unabashedly pissed-on beauties, drowning in torrents of apologies, would leave their phone numbers behind on torn-out sheets of notebook paper. Ignacy found these changes tiring at first, but he quickly came to find joy in them, and so one day in a letter to the previous owners he declared that he was prepared, should the need arise, to take the dog in indefinitely. And that's how it no doubt would have turned out, had it not been for a particular fall evening when the thing that Klara had always feared actually happened: Ignacy went for a walk that was undeniably too long.

This walk, which Klara learned about only much later, wouldn't have been such a surprise had it been, as Ignacy claimed, merely the logical consequence of a no longer bearable silence. No one grasped this better than Denisa. The moment Denisa first glimpsed the boy blundering through the labyrinth of paths was the same moment Ignacy first glimpsed the creature sitting on the park bench, engrossed in her book. Her face was tranquil, her gaze clear, and she embodied gentleness in a way typical of a woman who is no one's wife. Clever

Vaclav, following his master's thoughts, lost no time in running up to the bench and pissing all over not only her shoes but the legs of her pants, too, while Denisa merely peered over the top of her book and smiled with a serenity that should have become, in precisely that minute of autumn, the source of a hundred years' war. And that very night, though it would be another two weeks before the full moon, Ignacy went to the window and, to the consternation of a newly roused Vaclav Dragon, burst into tears. These were not, however, tears of redemption.

Along with the first snow, Klara came to notice unsettling gaps in Ignacy's letters. The narrow spaces between these gaps were filled with gems about his ongoing lack of time, rote confessions of devotion, and highly vague references to Vaclav Dragon's eccentric needs. Indeed, it seemed that Vaclav Dragon's needs were becoming increasingly demanding. He didn't like it when Ignacy left town, the sound of the telephone ringing at night disturbed him, and for all that he required ever longer walks and needed to take them not only during the day but late at night, too. Klara, detecting not so much a sick bladder as a sick heart, at one point got on the first morning train and, looking Ignacy straight in the eyes, asked him: "So who's the whore?" Caught off guard, Ignacy would have liked nothing better in that moment than to have never been born. At first he feigned surprise, then he insisted that Klara needed help, and in the end, pierced clean through by the daggers of her eyes, he blurted out the whole messy truth about the walks in the park. It was in part the same story that he had recounted in bits and pieces to Denisa, the story about his doggish life and dogged homelessness, about the pregnant silence, and the wild howling even without the moon.

And patient Denisa listened. Gentler than the grass, clear as any Cartesian cogitation, immune to thunder and lightning both, pensive, Denisa stroked Vaclav Dragon's muzzle, extracted a tick from his matted fur, and sighed: "What you need, Doggie, is a normal home." Her good-heartedness moved Ignacy to tears, and the warmth of her smile lulled to sleep both the pain of recent events and the fear-fractured thought of what was to come. But absent people don't have a voice, and born as she was under the sensible sign of Virgo, Denisa knew this. She also quite rightly rejected such abstract temporal categories like the past and firmly believed in the power of the here-and-now. She was a good listener, and at the same time, trusting the conventional playground wisdom that winners divulge nothing, she never betrayed herself in unnecessary remarks. Once she invited Ignacy home and, after pouring them both drinks and discreetly withdrawing into the shadows, stayed up until midnight listening with rapt attention to the story of this poet who fell prey to soulless piranhas. Squinting to hide her alarm, she replenished their snifters, and out of sheer earnestness, moved by the course of his catastrophes, loosened her hair from its bun. When he pressed her about her own fate, she pleaded triviality: her life could only seem boring in comparison to the abundance of Ignacy's. She only made allusions to the fact that of course she had happened to fall in love — ten whole years — but even though this man still sends her flowers every Tuesday, true love is invisible to her; true love, however, doesn't fall into the trap of blindness or cruelty. The most important thing in life, though, is friendship, she added, embarrassed, and to her own surprise, almost in spite of herself, pulled Ignacy's trembling hand to her breast.

But to be a best friend, she whispered at dawn, rubbing Ignacy's stomach, you have to want to be as close as possible, and isn't it strange that someone as exceptional as Klara can't see that. Ignacy quoted this last sentence to Klara as a reproach. He managed to get out of the way at the last minute, and the glass of wine shattered on the floor, splattering over Vaclav Dragon's bowl. Unfortunately, deprived of Denisa's invaluable attributes, nowhere near as rational and altogether too intense, Klara lost more with each furious explosion of abuse. Ignacy for his part, numb with horror, ended up doing something he certainly had never done before but had wanted to more than once: With all his might he punched Klara in the face. At that very moment Vaclav Dragon, who had just given up pursuit of his own tail, couldn't believe his eyes, and realizing that there was now no chance of still going on a walk that night, treaded his mat a few times and went to sleep.

Throughout the long months of winter Vaclav Dragon was the only inhabitant of those wardrobe-less two rooms who felt like he was happy. And it's hardly surprising: Denisa loved the big dog with all her heart; she picked him clean of all his ticks and whispered into his ear all the secrets of her simple soul. She thought about him constantly, made sure his walks were long and frequent, and once she even arranged an excursion to the country, where Vaclav Dragon, who was used to the rigors of the city, could pace the fields and forests. They became such good friends, in short, that by spring, when a completely broken-up Ignacy was thinking of initiating a repeat encounter with Klara, Denisa offered to take care of the dog herself. Her pure disinterestedness moved Ignacy so much that, for lack of any better idea, he kissed her on both cheeks, knelt down before her on his left knee, and vowed to give Vaclav Dragon as a present a bone the size of a baobab tree.

The memory of Denisa stayed with him for an entire week, and he simply couldn't handle her sudden absence. He looked at Klara in disgust and swore that she'd gotten uglier, that she wore too much lipstick, had lost her sense of humor, and who knew why she couldn't stop shaking, and how on her face in place of a bright morning smile there was a spider web of fear. It looked like she'd been abandoned by that disarming vanity of hers, too, which, if only it hadn't happened, once led him to fall in love with her in an airport mirror. He had a hard time recognizing in Klara the woman he would talk about in tears at daybreak, and whose history Denisa had memorized. So shouldn't she, Denisa, have been the cause for wonder? Shouldn't he have loved her, her loyalty, her good-heartedness, her unbounded "yes," and her eternal devotion? Denisa's serenity turned him on as much as it gave him pause. How fucking normal could that be, he thought, not to be completely overcome with jealousy? Does she have any emotions at all? Or maybe it's like Klara says, and she really does spend the night sticking pins into a little wax doll of her.

Ignacy's head pounded with these questions until the day Klara placed a bouquet of lilies of the valley on the table along with a dinner that she had made herself. She looked pretty; exhaustion had given her the chapped countenance of an icon, and her hands simply trembled with their fervor to be kissed. She did not eat much, picking at her cauliflower like a bird, and Ignacy, feeling tenderness entering his heart, put down his fork, took Klara in his arms, and unable to hold out for the bed, made love to her on the rug in the hallway. At the end of two weeks he was cured of his doubts and although he still preferred not to talk about the future, the present ceased tormenting him with every dawn they greeted together. Days they spent mainly taking walks in the woods. Ignacy carved hearts in the bark of trees, Klara fed the ducks, and whenever a couple of old people passed by, they would clasp their hands together and gaze into each other's eyes, smoldering with a silence fueled by their racing associations. I'd like it if you were white there, whispered Ignacy. And I'd like it if you were bald there, Klara laughed and nibbled Ignacy's finger. They were happy as never before, and the embarrassing memory of Denisa reared its head only when Klara, tired from walking, slipped into an occasional late-night delirium. This is why it was after several months, as he was looking out the window of a train, that Ignacy realized much to his shame that he hadn't bought Vaclav Dragon the present he'd promised, the bone large as a baobab tree.

Vaclav Dragon wasn't especially upset about it. He'd put on weight, he'd grown, and was doing really well, with the possible exception of his stubborn habit of throwing himself after bitches, sticks, and people. He had even bitten Denisa on the calf once, which was, Klara flatly declared, a way of punishing her for whoring around, and which Ignacy, for peace's sake, chose not to comment on. No one knew how it really happened that one day Vaclav Dragon disappeared. Klara, who in her heart often had wished him dead, felt just rotten about it, she didn't even suggest buying a new puppy, realizing it would have been unnecessarily masochistic to do so. Ignacy never brought it up anyway, and the dog disappeared from his letters just as ruthlessly as if he had never been there.

Only Denisa spent some time wandering around the park, lost in thought. "Vaclav! Come back!" she would call out, angrily throw the stick, and stop by one of the benches where she sat and smoked one cigarette after the other. But once she began taking care of a cat she'd found blundering through the labyrinth of life, she stopped thinking about him.

kumari

At a quarter of nine as usual Margarita got out of bed and shuffled sleepily into the bathroom, stumbling over books and shoes on the way. The mildewy dampness of the towels irritated her feet, the remains of her toothbrush bristled sadly, and the soap spilled over the rim of the soap dish in a gluey white cataract into the sink. Margarita bravely looked herself in the eye. They were the eyes of a soul, black precipitous spots, two suns eclipsed just as prophecy foretold.

Although he was in good health and did not lack for attributes, Hector was a melancholy and eternally pensive young man. But people tended to like him, just as they tend to like clouds, and as he also could play the guitar quite beautifully, women would stop outside his window, dreamily stroke their bare necks, and volley prickly little balls of sighs into his room. Hector revered women, and although he considered it debauchery to kiss a lady's hand, he always gave up his seat for them in the tram and would writhe in torment whenever they cried on his account. Unfortunately, they cried often, and the reason for this, as he himself would admit, was his tendency not to finish things, a tendency stronger than his own will. He was not particularly attached to them, but he still would not turn any of them away, and so in time his life, which should have been simple and quiet, began to resemble a riotous pageant of sobs untethered from their chain, proliferating without cause or aim.

Ill-disposed to the monotonies of gratification, Hector wanted to meet a woman who had yet to take leave of her senses on account of love, whose conquest would culminate not in a one-time seizure, but in a secret trail leading to endlessly higher summits. A woman like that, as everyone knows, is a fourth wonder of the world (along with monogamy, hirsute teeth, and truth that doesn't hurt), and can occur only when a series of necessary conditions have first been satisfied.

He who gauges his strength to his objective, Icarus excepted, has wings to fly with.

As for Hector, his problems were quite serious. One particular evening in spring, on his way back from an apartment where he had been welcome to stay, of course, and, without a thought for the consequences, to leave at daybreak, on this particular evening then, returning all by himself between park benches creaking with love, Hector came to the conclusion that he was a person of above-average nobility. This recognition in a way put him under two obligations: primo, to be a model of respectability, and secundo, to be intrepid in his judgments. Respectability, one may presume, comes with age; judgment, however, considering the nature of certain cravings, should not be unduly postponed.

Hector knew this, and although this knowledge long remained purely theoretical, it one day happened, and it was summer and the birds were singing more beautifully than an emperor's nightingale, and on this particular day, standing in a corner of Bar Globus, was a woman, whom a certain author in his wistful lunacy was bound to name Margarita. She was dressed gracefully, her hair styled modestly, and her hands, like two skiffs on rough seas, undulated in the air, hovering nimbly over her stately head, and then, as if ashamed of their freedom, drifted meekly down to her hips. Hector's eyes glazed over with the certainty he had long looked forward to. Spellbound by her hands' ballet, he rose slowly from his chair, approached the woman and, picking her up and setting her on the table in one deft move, whispered: "I have walked so many roads, all to become a man, but how can a man live without God?"

Chosen out of hundreds and elevated to Parnassus completely unprepared, Margarita started to laugh. Hector was not mistaken: She had never loved, or at any rate, she had never been madly in love. She toyed with feelings as nonchalantly as a cat, and never even noticed how deceptively easy unrequited love could be. Roses delighted her. She ate their petals and afterwards spit them out on sheets of poetry while with the sweetest of smiles entertaining ludicrous attempts to woo her. Time for the idolized flows carefree and fleet. After two years, which passed in a twinkling, an unresisting Margarita allowed herself to be led to a two-chamber palace. Awaiting her there was a throne and crimson vestments and a dozen bottles of wine more potent than aged. Hector took a black crayon from the drawer and around her large eyes drew eyes even larger. "I will love you forever," he swore, "or at any rate, for as long as my love doesn't blind you." But these words, which were the key to eternal happiness, unfortunately missed the ear of the many-eyed goddess.

The first few months on her throne were fun ones for Margarita. Mornings Hector woke her with a kiss, brought her coffee and a little bowl of salad in bed, and caressing her arms and hair all morning long, told her of his love. Afterwards, he bathed and dressed her, thought up new names for her, turned the most elaborate somersaults, and read the newspaper aloud. Afternoons, they washed down their dinner with wine, and evenings, as Margarita was sinking into slumber, Hector cracked the whip, and they mounted their steed and heedless of the road signs sped off for the cinema. Revived, Margarita would laugh until her eyes filled with tears. Wilder than the horse and glaring fiercely at the road, Hector looked exhilaratingly beautiful, and his love and devotion agreeably stroked her elect, idolized vanity. Unfortunately, while love indeed has wings, an excess of it will only clip them, and so with time Hector's flights peaked at ever-lower altitudes.

For Margarita was growing bored. The litany of declarations, the liturgy and laments, the heavenly chariots, the somersaults and burnt offerings, and the unbearable monotony of sainthood became increasingly oppressive. Incensed and alienated, with a foot propped up on Hector's back, she filed her nails for hours in silence, and although Hector had lost both his appetite and his senses, his despair did not so much move her as awaken in her an inclination to truly divine atrocities. To what tests did she subject his defenseless emotions! With an insouciance typical of those loved to excess, she exacted sacrifices so far-fetched that in compliance with her cruel desires Hector slaughtered at the base of her throne his most secret dreams, his worldly joy, and the remains of his dignity diced up like cabbage.

He might have taken this opportunity to sacrifice his entire earthly existence, to transcend the limits of his body and dissolve in a rainbow of colors free of illusions. But that is not what happened. After all, even the gods are mortal, and as scripture has it, a week before they die, they already start to smell with the terrible stench of their own end.

One day, Margarita restlessly began opening the windows. But although she lit incense, had her body rubbed down with rose oil, and roasted an orange peel over a candle flame, the stench would not abate. Alarmed, Hector flung open the windows and sitting on the sill with a handkerchief to his nose, noticed to his surprise what a sunny day it was, and that the birds alighting on the flowering magnolia sang more beautifully than an emperor's nightingale. A girl with a basket of apples smiled at the pale youth, stopped under his window, hummed a few bars of a song, and ran off, leaving her handkerchief behind. The song was cheerful and called back to life the desires curled up on the floor of Hector's heart, and the handkerchief was fragrant with a new certainty to look forward to.

"Let's saddle up the horse and go to the movies," Margarita suggested quietly. She slid hesitantly off her throne and tried to hug him. But Hector had grown to giant proportions and eluded every embrace. He kept growing, larger than the palace itself, and began to pour out the windows and doors, and as soon as he outgrew the injustice he had suffered, he cast the blubbering Margarita a blank look, set the girl with the basket of apples on the table, and picking the strings of his guitar, sighed: *La déesse est morte; vive la déesse.*

the final blow

She gave the plants some water, and then she drank some tea.

She was dying, but not even the table knew it. The table stood as it always had next to the wall, wooden for generations and more worm-eaten than Marian. Immune to changes in temperature, it stood there impassively.

"Marian," she sighed. "Marian." But Marian did not hear her. Not only was Marian farther away than the table, he was deafer than the table, too.

All the same, she waited. In her virginal purity she was convinced that Marian would hear her thoughts, jump up from his desk, come running to her, and fall at last to his knees, sobbing: "Paulina, I've loved you for forty-seven years, be my wife." And then, knowing she was dying anyway, she would look at him lovingly and whisper: "No, my sweetest, I love you too much to make you a widower."

But Marian did not come.

Attempting to extinguish the last of her illusions, Paulina overcame her pride for the last time, dialed Marian's telephone number, and whispered: "Marry me, darling."

the chosen one

A state of permanent frustration had gouged four lines into Theodore's pretty face: two vertical ones that practically encompassed his mouth and two horizontal ones on his forehead. Branded with sadness, this deeply expressive and even more deeply inscrutable face attracted the attentions of women, especially those who told fortunes. Reading the lines in people's faces was what Maya, a.k.a. "Princess," did.

"You're in love with a woman you're about to meet," Maya mumbled, applying incense to one of the lines. "It will be total love: Holy as Heaven, depraved as Hell, and unreal as Earth."

"Really?" Theodore perked up; he in fact relished depravity and already was wishing for a change of some sort. "And where will I meet her?"

"You'll meet her in a strange place very far from here," Maya sighed. "Fortunately, I won't be there."

Before Theodore could express surprise, Maya pulled a turtle out of her bag.

"Show him what he has to look forward to!" she demanded in a loud voice, and at once there appeared on the turtle's shell, as if on a miniature movie-screen, scenes of agony that would have been unimaginable even for late Kurosawa. The earth stood not in flames — the earth succumbed to cold. For although the temperatures were rising, the deserts were covered in frost and the only flower to survive was a computer-generated hibiscus. The books had been burned, the noses of Buddhas hacked off, and on the ruins of monasteries atomic reactors erected. Seeing all this, the Nordic races grew even paler and went blind from fear. The last monarchies were toppled, and on the social map there appeared, in place of princesses, moist spots, scabs, and a handful of coronets up for sale.

Theodore's eyes widened.

"And that's what it will be like when I meet her?" he asked in astonishment.

"It sure looks like it," Maya shrugged her shoulders. "Of course, you can always take my words for so much millennial gibberish, but I don't think that will change anything," she added, wrapped the turtle in a rag, and vanished with a sigh of relief.

Lost in thought, Theodore walked to the window and tried, peeping at the midsummer sky, to imagine having sex on a frost-covered mattress.

art diabolica

> *I turn round*
> *Like a dumb beast in a show,*
> *Neither know what I am*
> *Nor where to go*
> *— W.B. Yeats*

The black man could tell that I had not been in New York for a long time.

"Hey, where are you from?" he starts up just after the first corner.

"From Prague," I answer right away. I squint and wait for his confusion.

"From Prague?" the black man repeats, confused. "Prague, Prague . . . Where is that exactly?"

"It's in Europe," I say.

He examines me carefully in his mirror.

"Europe," he says, "you mean, on the other side of the ocean?"

"Yep, on the other side of the ocean," I say. This rouses him.

"Hot damn! So what do you do over there in Prague?" he shouts.

Good question, I think to myself and hesitate a moment. Really, what is it that I do over there in Prague?

"I guess I'm what you'd call a writer," I blurt out all of a sudden and we both start laughing.

"A writer, huh?" the black man repeats. "You mean, poetry, stuff like that?"

"Exactly," I say. "Poetry, stuff like that."

"Jesus, brother, that is the shit!" he roars and slaps his thighs. "You really went all the way over the ocean just to write some poems? You go, poet!"

"Former poet," I correct him and reassert my composure. "Since I've been away, I've written nothing but letters."

The black man keeps smiling.

"Letters," he says chuckling. "So what's wrong with letters? Hey, did you know Bob?" he asks. "Everyone knew him: Bob Robin, the world's biggest asshole. He'd fuck everyone but his own wife. 'I respect her too much,' he said."

The black man lights a cigarette and suddenly stops talking.

"So what about him?" I ask.

"He damn well fell off a roof is what he did, and on his own birthday, too. And there on the table, do you know what he left behind on the table?"

I have no idea.

"He left a poem on the table."

The black man slows down, lowers his eyelids, and begins to recite:

> *The king refused to bow his head*
> *They had to break his neck*
> *So he could look down at his stomach*
> *Which everyone says was full*
> *Of the grumbling truth*

"Don't you get it?" he asks.

I don't. The man laughs.

"I made it up," he says. "I made up Robin, too. It's my poem. Or the start of one."

"But you can't force it," he says and puts his foot on the gas. "A poem has got to grow inside you. And once it's all grown, then you'll see how you never have to write it down."

Now I'm the one staring.

"I'm a poet," the black man explains. "It's just I don't write. I'm a sonofabitch with no way to express myself. I'm a monster, brother, and I don't intend to have to justify myself."

Welcome to the club, I think. The black man is just getting warmed up.

"Because when you do something, brother, when you write something, you have to have some kind of reason for it, right?" he says. "But there are reasons everywhere, life is littered with reasons. The problem is, you don't always have enough nerve, if you have any at all, to recognize the reason when you see it. Most of the time you act as if the reason doesn't exist, so you write for no reason at all. You're in denial. You're in denial because you don't have the nerve to connect with it. You keep paying attention to things you don't have any connection to, you go to the park and write poems about the locust trees. Or you write a description of a portico, or a cathedral, or an altar. The more demons you have inside you, the more you use the word 'angel.' And your wife starts looking more and more like a cauliflower, too."

I stare dumbfounded at the back of the man's neck.

"Where did the cauliflower come from?" I ask.

"From the earth," the black man says. "Everything comes from the earth: Cauliflower, women, poetry. When you have the nerve to recognize that for what it is, then you're ripe for a poem. But when you're afraid, then you wither and die in your own fake garden. You die slowly and blame your death on your wife. Do you have a wife? I don't," he says. "But I used to. Grace. She was really beautiful. I loved her, brother, Jesus did I ever love her. She was good as gold, we never ever fought. It was like we were living in paradise, except that inside me something started growing, something evil. It was a shame, brother, a huge shame. Grace was so good it made me want to beat her sometimes. I never did actually hit her, but I started losing sleep over the thought that I could. Her little blue boots, they were tormenting me night and day, know what I mean? Velvety, soft, completely innocent. Those damned boots provoked me. And if it wasn't the boots, it was her bright yellow blouse. Or the gold chain around her neck. Even her belly button. I don't know how to explain it, I was crazy in love with her, but just the sight of her woke up the monster inside me. I started terrorizing her, only in my thoughts of course, but there must have been something in my eyes, too, because once I saw how Grace was watching me completely terrified. I asked her if she was scared of me, and then I twisted her arm around so hard the pain made her shout and start to cry. I was up all night after that; I tried praying, but the monster wouldn't get out. If I'd had the nerve back then to recognize that monster for what it was, maybe everything would have turned out different. But what's done is done. I appeased him. But maybe I was just testing the limits of my own hypocrisy, who knows. The more I loved Grace, the more I hated her. She was destroying me without even knowing it."

The black man wipes his forehead.

"I'm not sure I understand you," I admit.

"You see, brother," he says after a moment, "women are always a challenge at first, and sometimes they stay that way to the end. But usually they don't. Usually a woman is like a cross-bar that always stays at the same height. Whether you jump over it once, twice, or fifty times, it doesn't matter, it always stays the same. Always the same applause and fried bananas. Routine, brother, routine is the bomb that blows up on the thousandth episode of a TV show. Some people can put up with it. But I can tell you're not one of them. You're someone who needs to keep jumping higher, even if it means breaking every bone in your body. You need to destroy, you need to feel pain. You need the evil in order to feel the good, otherwise you'd go crazy. Am I right? I know I am," he laughs, "I'm a poet."

"So what happened to Grace?" I ask.

"The good Lord took her from me," he sighs, "The good Lord gave her to an attorney on Wall Street," he adds, and we both start laughing.

"You know," I say, "before, when I was still in school, I used to write poems. I sent them to Brodsky, and do you know what? He wrote back to me. That is, he sent me back my poems, all marked up like a homework assignment, but then he told me he was waiting for the next ones. That was like an initiation for me, and ever since I've thought of myself as a real writer. Not long after that, though, something terrible happened. I was living in Washington, D.C., and my girlfriend at the time, who was German, went away for a month to Köln. I admit, I didn't miss her much, I have some problems with Germans. Maybe I was even happy she was gone. At night I would go to the bars by myself, of course I always had my notebook and pencil with me, I'd order a whisky and scribble something in the notebook that later on I would try turning into a poem. There was a woman who worked in this bar, a Mexican woman. She had a good twenty years on me, she wasn't exactly pretty, but there was something, you know, genuine about her, and she was definitely a hothead. She lived on my street, but I never saw her during the day. She spoke with a funny accent and was always fiddling with her bracelet. The few times I allowed myself to take long walks with her, we'd sit on park benches and I would listen to her tell me all about her bisexual husband and caress her hands until dawn. You know what I mean, young poets love situations like that. Later on, at home, I'd jot down her words in my notebook and give them my own endings. Of course, I sensed a spark of something in her right from the beginning; it even provided me with a kind of pleasure. But one night she practically made my blood freeze in my veins, I'm serious. She came over to my table, and instead of sitting down like she usually did, she just stood there and laid into me about how she'd had enough of my games and that it was time for me to get to the point. I don't know what I was feeling then, I only remember that I didn't even bother to close my notebook. I didn't even look at her, I just began acting like I was writing something. She shoved me in the shoulder. I stopped writing and just smiled at her, you know what I mean; it must have been one of those smiles that drive women to murder. But this woman had been around and she didn't kill me. All she did was tell me, or actually hiss at me, that she'd be waiting for me at home in one hour. So you see, that's when I raised my eyebrows and looked at her like I was an angel being raped, and politely asked her not to be absurd. 'Anna, don't be absurd,' is what I said. Then she made some kind of an inhuman noise, backhanded the ashtray off the table, pointed at the door, and screamed about what fucking trash I was and how she never wanted to see me again. I walked out, I remember, without a word. I went back to my apartment and began rummaging through my poems. I was completely calm. Darling, I thought, you'll go begging for the love of a poet yet. That's exactly what I was thinking, and I knew I was right. I picked out one of my poems, copied it onto a sheet of paper, and then walked barefoot down the street and slipped it under her doormat. I knew she would get off work at three a.m. At four you'll call, I thought, and went back home and turned on the television. At five of four the phone rang. 'I want you,' is all she said. 'I'm waiting,' I said. And she came, with my poem in hand. She was totally limp, I led her to the bed, undressed her. All of a sudden something happened. With me. I don't know how to explain it to you, but suddenly I felt like a demon. Like a demon abusing his powers. Like a poet misusing his talent. How can I say this, I felt powerful beyond my own strength. I sat on the bed, turned off the light, and she started crying. She cried without saying anything, and I sat next to her, cold as stone, incapable of the slightest gesture. Finally she asked me if she could spend the night. 'Of course,' I said. I left her naked under the comforter and took a blanket with me to the couch in the other room. I can't remember when I fell asleep, but by seven in the morning she was already gone. I never saw her again, and I thought then that with time I would forget all about it. But no, with time I find myself remembering her more and more."

The black man doesn't say anything. He lights a cigarette, makes a left turn, and stops in front of Eveline's house.

"That's just the beginning, you know that," he says, tossing my banknote into a rusty box, and drives off.

translator's note

Few Polish prose writers of the past ten years have attracted as much delight and bewilderment as Natasza Goerke. Her stories, which are commonly fastened with predicates like "surreal," "grotesque," "ludicrous," "ironic," and "extravagant," call to mind the absurdist and parabolic traditions of Daniil Kharms, Cristina Peri Rossi, Sławomir Mrożek, Juan Carlos Onetti, Clarice Lispector, and Antonio Tabucchi. Although her reluctance toward straightforward narration, her refusal of any "responsibility" on the part of the writer to provide metaphysical product for the national masses, and her involvement with esoteric perspectives such as Buddhism and Asian cultures generally, all have caused less avant-garde-friendly critics to shake their heads in consternation, her erudition and extremely fine feeling for the Polish language have earned her recognition from all quarters as one of the most innovative and important voices of the younger generation.

Natasza Goerke's life often serves as grist for literary rumor mills in Poland, but a few facts can be discerned with relative certainty. She was born to assimilated Jewish parents in Poznań in 1960. She studied Polish in Poznań and Sanskrit in Kraków in the mid-1980s before leaving Poland in 1984. After a year in Copenhagen, she settled in Hamburg, where she now lives. She has also spent considerable time in India and Nepal. Her first stories appeared in Poland in journals such as *Czas Kultury* and *bruLion*, which in the early 1990s promoted the often-turbulent emergence of younger writers into the literary public sphere. Her first book, *Fractale* (Fractals) was published in 1994 to immediate acclaim; and two equally successful books have since followed: *Księga Pasztetów* (The Book of Patés) in 1997, and *Pożegnania Plazmy* (Farewells to Plasma) in 1999. The parabolic short pieces of the first book gave way in the second to longer, more developed narratives and greater experimentation with time and form. The third has continued this trend, with playful experiments in genre and narrative links between stories. With their torsions of narrative and syntax, hairpin shifts in register and resonance, and often bizarre humor, the stories in these books betoken a contemporary invigoration of the short form in prose, and not only within the context of Polish letters. The same humor and confidence in her language's own current characterize Goerke's writing process, too: "Occasionally I know ahead of time, very foggily, what I want to write; then the rest of the story comes while I'm writing. Sometimes I laugh myself to tears before I've put even one word down on paper, which is a good sign . . ."[1]

While English sentences can, contrary to commonplace, accommodate syntax as condensed as Goerke's often is, the rapid itinerary of her imagination across such a jagged terrain of linguistic and literary specificities is a hard one to reconstruct. Words and phrases that bristle and chime in one culture are often impossible to transport into another without sounding sterile and flat. And even then, one must first have perceived the original resonance. I owe much of the precision of this translation to Kinga Maciejewska, who vetted the entire manuscript, as well as to Piotr Siemion and Alicja Jankowska, who were kind enough to read and provide helpful suggestions on "La Mala Hora" and "Dog," respectively. I also have consulted Hans-Peter Hoelscher-Obermaier's excellent German rendering of Goerke's last book for confirmation or correction of my translations of the same texts.

Theories of translation have increased hundredfold in the last decade, but in terms of the actual parameters of practice, little has changed since Dryden and Schleiermacher. I have tried to remain as

---

[1] Petra Schellen, "Heiligsein ist öde ... und fast unerträglich, findet die groteskenfreudige polnische Autorin Natasza Goerke, die jetzt in Hamburg liest. Ein Porträt," *Die TAZ* (Hamburg), 12 Oct. 2000, p. 1.

faithful to these texts as possible, while at the same time upholding my necessary commitments to English. On this score I would like to express my gratitude to Eric P. Elshtain and Eirik Steinhoff for their editorial suggestions and encouragement; and to Jeffrey Young for his careful and committed editorship, especially for his contributions to "For the Sake of Art," and for introducing me to Natasza's work in the first place. Special thanks are due to Howard Sidenberg, for his dedication to publishing translations of Central European literature in general and to this project in particular.

W. Martin
Berkeley, June 2001

about the author

Natasza Goerke was born in Poznań in 1960. She studied Polish at Mickiewicz University in Poznań and Oriental Languages at Jagiellonian University in Kraków. In the mid-1980s she emigrated from Poland and, after having lived for a time in Asia, she took up residence in Hamburg, Germany. She has published three books in Polish and two collections in German translation, both of which received critical acclaim. Her stories have appeared in numerous magazines in Poland and in the Polish émigré press, with translations appearing in magazines and anthologies in Slovenian, Macedonian, Serbo-Croatian, Flemish, German, and English (*The Eagle and the Crow*, Serpent's Tail, 1996). In 1993 she received the Czas Kultury Prize and in 1995 she was awarded a six-month stipendium at the prestigious Akademie Schloss Solitude outside of Stuttgart, the only Polish writer thus far to have received this distinction.

about the translator

W. Martin is a doctoral student in Comparative Literature at the University of Chicago. He teaches in the Writing Program of the School of the Art Institute of Chicago, and is fiction editor of *Chicago Review*, for which he guest-edited a special issue (Fall 2000) on Polish literature in the nineties.

FAREWELLS TO PLASMA by Natasza Goerke
Translated from the Polish by W. Martin
Designed by H&H Design
The selection in this volume was taken from the following collections:
Fractale (Poznań: Obserwator, 1994); *Księga Pasztetów* (Poznań: Obserwator, 1997); *Pożegnania plazmy* (Gładyszów: Czarne, 1999). "Waiting Underground (Transitions)" was published in the original under the same title in the magazine *Przekładaniec* (2000).
This is a first edition published in 2001 by Twisted Spoon Press
P.O. Box 21, Preslova 12, 150 21 Prague 5, Czech Republic
www.twistedspoon.com / info@twistedspoon.com
Printed and bound in the Czech Republic by Tiskárny Havlíčkův Brod
Available to the trade in North America through SCB Distributors
15608 South New Century Drive, Gardena, CA 90248;
1-800-729-6423 / info@scbdistributors.com

ACKNOWLEDGMENTS:
Special thanks to Thomas A. Kostelac and Hana Huncovská for their help. Earlier versions of these stories have appeared previously in *Chicago Review*, *Conjunctions*, *Descant*, and *Trafika*.

"We must reach the pumpkin patch before sunset!"